100 Reasons to Celebrate

We invite you to join us in celebrating
Mills & Boon's centenary. Gerald Mills and
Charles Boon founded Mills & Boon Limited
in 1908 and opened offices in London's Covent
Garden. Since then, Mills & Boon has become
a hallmark for romantic fiction, recognised
around the world.

We're proud of our 100 years of publishing
excellence, which wouldn't have been achieved
without the loyalty and enthusiasm of our
authors and readers.

Thank you!

Each month throughout the year there will
be something new and exciting to mark the
centenary, so watch for your favourite authors,
captivating new stories, special limited
edition collections…and more!

Dear Reader

This year we celebrate the centenary of this wonderful publisher I write for. Since the time I fell in love with my first romance novel—ooh, when I was about thirteen—Mills & Boon romances have been giving me fun, fantasy, and a lovely escape now and then, when life gets a bit gritty. It's now my absolute honour to be giving pleasure by writing as well as receiving pleasure by reading.

Royal romances have always been a particular favourite, and in this, my centenary romance, I've made sure to give you the full fairytale. Prince Nikolai de Montez and Princess Rose Anitra McCray are everything a royal couple should be. Nik's gorgeous, charming, and noble. Rose is a country veterinarian, bogged down in the mud and sleet of a Yorkshire winter, just waiting for her Prince Charming to wave his magic wand—or at least find a tractor and haul her out of the mud. They're a match made in heaven, and they have a country to save.

My fairytale countries are the four Alp Countries. They're close to France and Italy (let's not be too specific, here) and straight out of Hans Christian Anderson. They have gleaming stone castles, snow-capped mountains, goat herds on high pastures—everything good principalities need. But the countries' economies are in ruin and the people are desperate. Nik and Rose are facing real problems and deadly danger as they fall in love.

Readers who've found my books in the past will recognise Nikolai as one of Ruby's boys—Ruby is the foster mother in my Dolphin Bay books. My characters intertwine between my stories—the residents of my castle at Dolphin Bay, the royal families of my Alp countries and my princes and princesses in waiting.

Writing romances is a joy, and I invite you to share my pleasure as millions have enjoyed Mills & Boon romances since 1908. This company and its loyal readers are a legend. Here's to the next hundred fabulous years.

Marion Lennox
www.marionlennox.com

A ROYAL MARRIAGE OF CONVENIENCE

BY
MARION LENNOX

MILLS & BOON

Pure reading pleasure

First published in Great Britain 2008
Harlequin Mills & Boon Limited,
Eton House, 18-24 Paradise Road, Richmond, Surrey TW9 1SR

© Marion Lennox 2008

ISBN: 978 0 263 86500 4

Set in Times Roman 13 on 14 pt
02-0308-50261

Printed and bound in Spain
by Litografia Rosés, S.A., Barcelona

Marion Lennox is a country girl, born on an Australian dairy farm. She moved on—mostly because the cows just weren't interested in her stories! Married to a 'very special doctor', Marion writes Medical™ Romances as well as Mills & Boon® Romance (she used a different name for each series for a while—if you're looking for her past Mills & Boon romances, search for author Trisha David as well). She's now had seventy romance novels accepted for publication.

In her non-writing life Marion cares for kids, cats, dogs, chooks and goldfish. She travels, she fights her rampant garden (she's losing) and her house dust (she's lost).

Having spun in circles for the first part of her life, she's now stepped back from her 'other' career, which was teaching statistics at her local university. Finally she's reprioritised her life, figured out what's important and discovered the joys of deep baths, romance and chocolate.

Preferably all at the same time!

This is Marion's 70th book!

BY ROYAL APPOINTMENT

You're invited to a royal wedding!

From turreted castles to picturesque palaces—these kingdoms may be steeped in tradition, but romance always rules!

So don't miss your VIP invite to the most extravagant weddings of the year!

Your royal carriage awaits...

Don't miss future books in this wonderful miniseries!

Coming in June from Mills & Boon Romance®
Her Royal Wedding Wish
by Cara Colter

CHAPTER ONE

'ROSE-ANITRA, we have a surprise for you.'

Rose sighed. In her experience surprises from her in-laws were like surprises in a fairground ghost-train: 'Surprise!' followed by green slime—or worse. Rose had spent the evening on a windswept scree, delivering a calf which had taken one look at the outside world and elected to stay put. It had taken her hours to persuade it to change its mind. She'd been up before dawn and she hadn't stopped since. More than anything else in the whole world, she wanted to go to bed.

There was also the issue of the letter. The stiff, formal communication had arrived, registered mail, in the midst of a bunch of condolence cards. She'd read it briefly, then had stuffed it in her overall pocket to try and make sense of later. She'd like to think about it now, but Rose knew better than to try and deflect her in-laws. So she perched on the edge of an overstuffed chair in their overheated sitting room, she clasped her hands obediently, and she braced herself.

'It's a wonderful surprise,' Gladys said, but for once she sounded a bit nervous.

'You'll be really pleased,' Bob said, and Rose cast him an uncertain glance. Ever since her husband Max had died two years ago, Rose suspected Bob empathised with her a little. But only a little. Not so much that he'd stand up to his wife.

'You know, it's the anniversary of Max's death today,' Gladys said, casting a quelling glance at her husband.

'Of course.' How could Rose have forgotten? Yes, she still grieved for the man she'd loved, but maybe it was a little over the top that her veterinary clinic had been filled with as many flowers today as it had been two years ago. Max had been a loved son of the village. His memory would be kept alive for ever.

'We waited until now to tell you,' Gladys said. 'Because Max asked us to wait. He said we were to let you get the worst of your grieving over, for you couldn't have coped with a child until now.'

'I… What are you saying?' Rose's fingers clenched involuntarily into her palms. Of course she couldn't have coped with a child. Not when she'd been fighting to earn her way though vet school. Not when she and Max had been battling his illness. And not now, when she was struggling to earn enough for this tiny vet clinic to support them all.

'But now it's time,' Gladys said, and she smiled.

'Time?' Rose managed. 'For what?'

'It's his sperm,' Bob said, and the elderly man's voice was eager. 'It's Max's sperm, Rose. When he first got sick, years and years ago, he was naught but a lad, but they told us that the treatment might make him infertile. Even then we thought who'd inherit this life? Who'd take this place forward?'

Who indeed? But Rose wasn't asking the question. She was staring at them in dawning horror.

'So we had it frozen,' Gladys said. 'And we wanted it to be a surprise. It's his two-year anniversary present. From Max to you. Now you can have his babies.'

Five hundred miles away in London, in the illustrious international law firm Goodman, Stern and Haddock, another surprise was being played out.

Nikolai de Montez, barrister-at-law, was staring at the elderly man across his desk in stunned silence.

He'd walked in five minutes before the scheduled appointment he'd made a week earlier, neatly dressed, stooped with age, and with hands that trembled. The card he'd handed over had said simply: *'Erhard Fritz. Assistant to the Crown.'*

'My question is simple, really,' Erhard said without preamble. 'If it meant you were to inherit a throne, would you be prepared to marry?'

As partner in this internationally renowned law firm, Nick was accustomed to listening to all sorts of outrageous proposals, but this was one to take the breath away.

'Would I be prepared to marry?' he said now, really carefully, as if his words alone could make the situation explode. 'May I ask…marry who?'

'A woman called Rose McCray. You might know her as Rose-Anitra de Montez. She's a veterinarian in Yorkshire, but it seems that she might also be first in line to the throne of Alp de Montez.'

How could she walk away? She couldn't, but for the last two days Rose had felt like she was walking in a nightmare—the nightmare that was the remains of her husband's life.

Everywhere she went she was surrounded by memories. She woke and Max looked down on her from the framed photograph beside their wedding bed. Gladys had collapsed in hysterics when Rose had wanted to give away his clothes, so Max's shirts and trousers still hung in the closet. Max's coats still hung in the entrance hall, his boots still stood on the back porch. 'I'll not be forgetting our Max,' she said fiercely when anyone challenged her.

Rose's grief over the death of her husband had been as deep as it had been sincere, but now it was starting to overwhelm her. She felt like she was living in a perpetual shrine to Max—and now they wanted her to have Max's child.

The request had been playing over and over in her head for the last two days—along with the contents of the letter. She was so weary she was about to fall over, but one truth was starting to emerge: this couldn't go on. Max had been dead these two years. If there'd been the money she would have moved out to a place of her own, but her income paid the upkeep on this place. She couldn't leave. Unless… Unless…

The proposal outlined in the letter was crazy, but so was this situation. The proposal was almost like a siren song. Alp de Montez…a country she loved. She lifted the photograph that had come with the letter, a picture of one Nikolai de Montez. He was long, lean and darkly handsome. His Mediterranean good looks were stunning.

He was about as different from Max as it was possible to get, she thought, reading the letter for the tenth time and then putting it firmly away. No. It was stupid. The letter was a lunacy, a crazy escape-clause with no guarantees that she wouldn't be worse off.

This was Max's community. She had to give it

one last try, no matter how trapped she was feeling. If only they'd back off about the baby.

She walked into the sitting room, determined to say what had to be said. They were waiting for her. Bob was pouring her a sherry.

'We've been thinking,' Gladys said before she could say a word. 'We're so excited about the baby, but you need to hurry. There's enough sperm for you to have more than one, and you're almost thirty. If you don't have a boy first, then we…' She caught herself. '*You'll* want another. Rose, we've made an appointment for you with the specialist in Newcastle tomorrow, and Bob's arranged for a locum so you can go.'

'That's good,' Rose said faintly, but she didn't take the sherry. Gladys smiled her approval.

'Good girl. I told Bob no alcohol. Not if you're pregnant.'

'I'm not pregnant yet.'

'But you will be.'

'No,' Rose said faintly, and then more forcibly. 'No. If you'll excuse me…' She took a deep breath. 'It's good that you've organised a locum. I need to go to London for a couple of days. I've received a letter.'

'A letter?'

'It came registered post to the surgery,' she said, knowing full well that any post out of the ordinary that came via the private letter-box was likely to be steamed open. 'You remember my family has royal connections?'

'Yes,' Gladys said, stiffening in disapproval.

'It seems someone came here to see me a week ago,' she said. 'Someone from Alp de Montez. You told him I was away?'

'I…' Gladys looked at Bob and then she looked at the carpet. 'He said he had a proposal for you,' she muttered, defensive. 'What would you be wanting with a proposal?'

Rose nodded. Two proposals in two weeks. The one facing her here made the other one seem mild in comparison.

But what Gladys had just said firmed things for her. If she agreed to have a child, a daughter would never be enough. If she finally had Max's son, then the child would be a living memorial to Max. What crazy reason was that to bring a child into the world?

'It seems I'm needed,' she said, thinking it through as she spoke. 'I mean…needed by some-one other than you. By someone other than my dead husband's family and his community. When I first read the letter I thought it was crazy, but it seems as if it's not crazy after all. Or no more crazy than this. Either way, I'm going to find out. I'm going to London to see if I've inherited a crown.'

CHAPTER TWO

THE restaurant Nick had organised as a rendez-vous was a good one. It was old-fashioned, full of oak wainscotting, linen table-cloths, and individual booths where people could talk without struggling to hear or worrying about being heard.

He walked in and Walter, the head waiter, met him with the familiarity of an old acquaintance. 'Good evening, Mr de Montez.' He looked at Nick's casual Chinos and cord jacket and he smiled. 'Well, well. Holiday mode tonight, then, sir?'

Holiday. Yeah, maybe this was his holiday. Nick hardly did holidays at all, so he might as well term this one. Oh, every now and then he'd fly back to Australia to see his foster mother, Ruby, with whom he kept in touch and phoned every Sunday without fail. He skied now and then with a few important clients, but mostly Nick lived to work. He was on holiday tonight because he'd donned casual clothes. That'd do him for while.

He was led over to the booth he generally used. Erhard was there already, and Nick appraised him more thoroughly as he rose to greet him. The old man looked thin, wiry and frail, with a shock of white hair and white bushy eyebrows. He was dressed in a deeply formal black suit.

'I'm sorry I wasn't here when you arrived,' Nick said, and he looked ruefully down at his clothes, regretting he hadn't opted for formal. 'And I'm sorry for these.'

'You think Rose-Anitra might be uncomfortable with formality?' Erhard asked, smiling.

'I did,' he confessed. Some time in the last few days, as Erhard had talked him through the situation, he'd handed over a photograph of Rose, taken a month ago by a private investigator. Rose had been working—the shot had her leaning against a battered four-wheel-drive vehicle, talking to someone out of frame. She was wearing dirty brown dungarees, Wellingtons and a liberal spray of mud. She was pale faced, with the odd freckle or six, and the only colour about her was the deep, glossy auburn of the braid hanging down her back.

She was a good-looking woman in a 'country hick' sort of way, Nick had conceded. The women in his world were usually sophisticated chic. There was no way this woman could be described in those terms, but she'd looked sort of…cute. So when dressing tonight he'd decided formal gear might make her uneasy.

'You may be underestimating her,' Erhard said.

'She's a country vet.'

'Yes. A trained veterinarian.' Still the hint of reproof. 'My sources say she's a woman of considerable intelligence.' And then he paused, for Walter was escorting someone to their table.

Rose-Anitra? The woman in the dungarees?

Nick could see the similarities, but only just. She was wearing a crimson, halter-necked dress, buttoned at the front from the below-knee hemline to a low-cut cleavage. The dress was cinched at the waist in a classic Marilyn Monroe style, showing her hourglass figure to perfection. Her hair was twisted into a casual knot, caught up with soft white ribands, and tiny tendrils were escaping every which way. She was wearing not much make-up—just enough to dust the freckles. Her lips were a soft rose, which should have clashed with her dress but didn't.

She was wearing stilettos. Gorgeous red stilettos that made her legs look as if they went on for ever.

'I believe I had it right,' Erhard said softly to him, and chuckled and moved forward to greet their guest. 'Mrs. McCray.'

'Rose,' she said and smiled, and her smile lit up the room. Her pert nose wrinkled a little. 'I think

I remember you. Monsieur Fritz—you were assistant to my uncle?'

'I was,' Erhard said, pleased. 'Please, call me Erhard.'

'Thank you,' she said gravely. 'It's been almost fifteen years, but I do remember.' She turned to Nick. 'And you must be Nikolai? Monsieur de Montez.'

'Nick.'

'I don't think I've met you.'

'No.'

Walter was holding out her seat and Rose was sitting, which hid her legs. Which was almost a national tragedy, Nick decided. What was she about, disguising those legs in dungarees? He surveyed her with unabashed pleasure as Walter fussed about them, taking orders, offering champagne. 'Yes, please,' Rose said, and beamed. When the champagne arrived she put her nose right into the bubbles and closed her eyes, as if it was her first drink for a very long time.

'You like champagne, then?' Nick said, fascinated, and she sighed a blissful smile.

'You have no idea. And it's not even sherry.' She had a couple more sips, then laid her glass back on the table with obvious reluctance.

'We're very pleased you were able to come,' Erhard said gently, and looked at Nick. 'Aren't we, Nick?'

'Yes,' said Nick, feeling winded.

'I'm sorry it took a while to contact me,' Rose told them, glancing round the restaurant with real appreciation. 'My family has an odd notion that I need protection.'

'You don't?' Nick asked.

'No,' she said, and took another almost defiant sip of champagne. 'Absolutely not. This is lovely.'

It was, Nick thought. She was.

'Maybe it'd be best if I outline the situation,' Erhard said, smiling faintly at Nick as if guessing his degree of confoundment. 'Rose, I'm not sure how much you know.'

'Not much at all,' she admitted. 'Only what you told me in the letter. The whole village seems to have been playing keepings off, from telling you I was away when you called, to refusing to pass on phone messages. If Ben at the post office hadn't been a man of integrity I might never have heard from you at all.'

'Why would they be worried about Erhard?' Nick asked, puzzled.

'My in-laws know I'm the daughter of minor royalty,' she said. 'My husband used to delight in it. But since he's died anything that might take me away from the village has been regarded with suspicion. I gather Erhard came, looked dignified and spoke with an accent. That'd be enough to make them worry. My in-laws have a lot of influence, and they don't like strangers. I'm sorry.'

'It's not your fault,' Erhard said gently. He hesitated. 'At least you're here now, which means that you may be prepared to listen. It might sound preposterous…'

'You don't know what preposterous is,' she said enigmatically. 'Try me.'

Erhard nodded. It seemed he was prepared to do the talking, which left Nick free to, well, just look.

'I'm not sure how much you know already,' Erhard said. 'I've talked the situation through with Nick this week, and I did outline this in the letter, but maybe I need to start at the beginning.'

'Go ahead,' Rose said, sipping some more champagne and smiling. It was an amazing smile. Stunning.

Nick was stunned.

Erhard cast him an amused glance. He was an astute man, was Erhard. The more Nick knew him, the more he respected him. Maybe he should look away from Rose. Maybe what he was thinking was showing in his face.

What the heck? Not to look would be criminal.

'I'm not sure if you know the history of Alp de Montez,' Erhard was saying, smiling between the pair of them. 'Let me give you a thumb sketch. Back in the sixteenth century, a king had five sons. The boys grew up warring, and the old king thought he'd pre-empt trouble. He carved four countries from his border, and told his younger sons that the cost of their own principality was lifelong allegiance to their oldest brother.

'But granting whole countries to warlike men is hardly a guarantee of wise rule. The princes and their descendants brought four wonderful countries to the brink of ruin.'

'But two are recovering,' Nick said, and Erhard nodded.

'Yes. Two are moving towards democracy, albeit with their sovereigns still in place. Of the remaining two, Alp de Montez seems the worst off. The old Prince—your mutual grandfather—left control more and more in the hands of the tiny council running the place. The chief of council is Jacques St. Ives, and he's had almost complete control for years. But the situation is dire. Taxes are through the roof. The country's on the brink of bankruptcy, and people are leaving in the thousands.'

'Where do you come into this?' Nick asked curiously. He knew much of this, and not all of it was second hand. Several years ago, curious about the country where his mother had been raised, he'd spent a week touring the place. What he'd seen had horrified him.

'I've been an aide to the old Prince for many

years,' Erhard said sadly. 'As he lost his health, I watched the power shift to Jacques. And then there were the deaths,'

'Deaths?' Rose asked.

'There have been many,' Erhard told her. 'The old Crown Prince died last year. He had four sons, and then a daughter. You'd think with five children there'd be someone to inherit, but, in order of succession, Gilen died young in a skiing accident, leaving no children. Gottfried died of a drug overdose when he was nineteen. Keifer drank himself to death, and Keifer's only son Konrad died in a car crash two weeks ago. Rose, your father Eric died four years back, and Nick, your mother Zia, the youngest of the five children, is also dead. Which leaves three grandchildren. Eric's daughters—you, Rose, and your sister Julianna—are now first and second in line for the throne. You, Nikolai, are third.'

'Did you know all this?' Nick asked Rose, and she shook her head.

'I knew my father was dead, but I didn't know any of the ascendancy stuff until I had Erhard's letter. My mother and I left Alp de Montez when I was fifteen. Have you ever been there?'

'I skied there once,' Nick admitted.

'Does that mean you can inherit the throne?' she asked, smiling. 'Because you skied there?'

'It almost comes down to that,' Erhard said,

and Nick had to stop smiling at Rose for a minute and look serious. Which was really hard. He was starting to feel like a moonstruck teenager, and he'd only had half a beer. Maybe he'd better switch to mineral water like Erhard.

But, regardless of what he was feeling, Erhard was moving on. 'We need a sovereign,' he said. 'The constitution of the Alp countries means no change can take place without the overarching approval of the Crown. I'd love to see the place as a democracy, but that's only going to happen with royal approval.'

'Which would be where we come in, I guess,' Rose said. 'Your letter said you needed me.'

'Yes.'

'But I'm not a real royal. Eric really wasn't my father.' She touched her flame-coloured hair and winced in rueful remembrance. 'Surely you remember the fuss, Erhard? Eric called my mother a whore and kicked her out of the country.'

'Not until you were fifteen. And you went with her,' Erhard said softly.

'There wasn't a lot of choice.' She shrugged. 'My sister—my half-sister—wanted to stay in the palace, but my mother was being cut off with nothing. There wasn't a lot of love lost between me and Julianna even then. My sister was jealous of me, and my father hated my hair. No. That's putting it too nicely. My father hated *me*. I had no place there.'

'He acknowledged you as his daughter until you were fifteen,' Erhard said. 'Yes, there was general consensus that you weren't his, but the people felt sorry for your mother, and they loved you.'

'And my grandfather wanted my mother in the castle,' Rose said bluntly. 'My grandfather didn't care about the scandal which had produced me. He knew his son was a womaniser, and he knew my mother's affair happened through loneliness. My mother was kind, in a family where kind was hard to get. It was only after Grandfather became so ill, and he wasn't noticing, that my father was able to send her away.'

'To nothing,' Erhard said bleakly. 'To no support.'

'We didn't care,' Rose said, sounding defiant. 'At least…it would have been nice at the end, but we got by.'

'So you left the throne for Julianna.'

'I didn't,' Rose said, sounding annoyed. 'My mother and I assumed Keifer and then Konrad would inherit. We weren't to know they'd die young.'

'So you've never officially removed yourself from the succession?'

'I didn't think I had to. If I'm not real royalty…'

'You *are* real royalty,' Erhard said, emphatic. 'You were born within a royal marriage.'

'I have red hair. No one in my extended family has red hair. And my mother admitted—'

'Your mother admitted nothing on paper.'

'But DNA…'

'If DNA testing were done, half the royal families of Europe would crumble,' Erhard told her. 'Your mother married young into a loveless marriage, but such things aren't unusual. Your parents are dead. There's no proof of anything.'

'Julianna looks royal.'

'You think?' Erhard asked, with a wry smile. 'There's no proof of that either, and no one dare suggest DNA. So we turn to the lawyers. There's an international jurisdiction—legal experts chosen for impartiality—set up by the four Alp principalities for just this eventuality. They decide who has best right to the crown. Rose, I told you in the letter, Julianna has married Jacques St. Ives and they're making a solid play for the crown. Their justification is that Julianna is the only one of the three of you who lives in the country, and moreover she's married to a citizen who cares about the place. You, Rose, walked away almost fifteen years ago. Regardless of your birth, your absence by choice sits as an implacable obstacle. The panel will decide in Julianna's favour, unless they're given an alternative.'

He hesitated. He looked as if he didn't want to continue—but it had to be said, and they all knew it. 'Rose, if there are questions about your parent-age there are also questions about Julianna's,' he said softly. 'Regardless of DNA testing, the panel acknowledge that. Your parents' marriage was hardly happy. You remain the oldest. And behind you both there's Nikolai, whose mother was definitely royal. I've thought and thought of this. The only way forward is for the two of you to present as one. Together you must outweigh Julianna's claim. A married couple—the questioned first and the definite third in line—taking on the throne together.'

Whatever Erhard had said in his letter, Rose must have been forewarned, Nick thought, as she was showing no shock. The idea had stunned him, but she was reacting as if it was almost reasonable. She sat and stared at the bubbles in her glass for a while, letting things settle. She wasn't a woman who needed to talk, he thought. The silence was almost comfortable.

'A marriage of convenience,' she said at last, as if the thing was worthy of consideration.

'Yes.'

'That's what I thought you meant after I read the letter. I guess it's why I came. It seemed that this way I might be able to help. But…' She smiled up at Walter as he delivered their meals, and she nodded absolute affirmation when he offered her wine. 'Are you sure Julianna and Jacques won't make good rulers?'

'I'm sure they won't,' Erhard said.

'Don't you know your sister?' Nick asked, curious.

'We were friends when we were little,' she said, sounding suddenly forlorn. 'Julianna was pretty and blonde and cute, and I was carrot-headed and pudgy. But despite that the old Prince liked me. He indulged me. He'd call me his little princess, and Julianna hated it. So did my father. It got so that I hated it too, and when it all blew up I was glad to go. I got to stay with my mother, my great-aunt and six crazy cats in London, while Julianna got to be a princess.' She gave a rueful smile. 'So she got what she wanted. But she never answered my letters or returned my calls. It was like she and my father just wiped us. You say she's married?'

'Yes,' Erhard said. 'To Jacques, who wants control of the throne.'

'I see.' She gave herself an irritated shake. 'I guess I expected no less. But how can I believe what you say of her intentions?'

'I can verify them,' Nick told her, feeling it was time he helped out. Erhard was looking so strained he looked like he might collapse. 'I've spent the last week researching the place. Alp de Montez is in serious trouble, and it will take a sovereign to help. There's never been the slightest interest in ruling the country properly from either Jacques, the presiding council, or from Julianna herself. Corruption is everywhere.'

'Oh,' Rose said in a small voice. She swallowed, and then suddenly seemed to make a conscious effort to shake off dreariness. 'This food is wonderful.'

It was wonderful. Nick had chosen steak, and somewhat to his surprise Rose had too. He was accustomed to women ordering something like grilled fish with a salad—or just a salad—and then not eating most of it, but there was none of the dainty eater about Rose. She tucked into her steak with enjoyment. There was a bowl of roast potatoes to share, fragrant with rosemary, and she reached for the last one before he did.

'Ladies first,' she said, and she smiled at him again, and the odd warmth he was feeling intensified.

Erhard, who had been the one to settle on grilled fish, chuckled quietly at the pair of them. 'This could be some match,' he said.

Hey, hold on. Nick jerked back to the issue at hand. He needed to put his hormones to one side and concentrate. 'We're far from deciding here,' he retorted. 'The thing seems a fairy tale.'

'None of us believe it's impossible, or we wouldn't be sitting here,' Erhard said smoothly. 'Rose thinks so too.'

'Rose isn't committing herself,' Rose retorted. 'I only said I'd meet him.'

'And you have met him, and he makes you smile.'

'Just because I beat him to the last potato. That's hardly a basis for a marriage.'

'Shared intelligence is a basis of a marriage,' Erhard said calmly. 'And shared compassion. Now I've met you both, I believe the thing might be possible.'

'Is there really no other way?' Nick said cautiously. But he wasn't feeling cautious. Ever since Erhard had walked into his office, a bubble of excitement had been growing inside him that refused to be suppressed. At first it had been the idea of having some say in turning around the fate of a nation. But now…

He'd never thought of marriage. Why should it be suddenly immensely appealing?

'Let's get this straight,' he said. 'Why not just Rose?'

Erhard nodded. He'd obviously prepared his responses very carefully.

'On the upside she's first in line, and once upon a time the people loved her,' he said. 'The downside is that as soon as the old Prince was unable to react Eric shouted from the rooftops that Rose wasn't his. Rose and her mother left the country fifteen years ago and never looked back.'

'Why not just Julianna, then?'

'On the upside, Julianna lives in the country and the people know her. But they don't like her. Or they don't like her husband, and Julianna does what her husband says. The inference that Rose isn't royal must also taint Julianna's claim. There's no proof. And Rose is older.'

'Why not just Nick, then?' Rose demanded.

'He's an unknown,' Erhard said flatly. 'I didn't know him myself until a week ago. He's been to the country as a tourist, but nothing else. The people will never accept him.'

'Maybe I could support Rose's claim without marriage,' Nick heard himself say, albeit reluctantly. There was a crazy voice in the back of his head saying 'take her and run'. He suppressed it with an effort. He had to be sensible. 'As someone in line myself, even if further away and the child of a royal daughter and not a son, I can surely add weight to Rose's position?'

'So can the President of our Council,' Erhard said bluntly. 'He supports Julianna. Julianna is a citizen of Alp de Montez, and she's married to another citizen. Rose was a people's favourite in the past. The press loved her, portraying her as a natural, friendly kid who always had a stray animal attached. But that knowledge of Rose has faded, and her father's vitriolic denunciation of her stands in her way. It will take a huge factor to swing the thing in Rose's favour. The only thing that will do it is your marriage.'

'And you?' Nick said, turning to Rose, puzzled. There was so much about this woman he didn't understand. 'You'd seriously consider marriage to gain a throne?'

She froze at that. She'd been smiling, but now her face stilled.

'Whoa,' she said. 'Let's not paint me a gold-digger.'

'I never said…'

'Yes, you did,' she said bluntly. 'So let's get things clear. Erhard's letter made me think. I'm not the least bit interested in playing the Crown Princess—that was always Julianna's preferred option—but there's not so many times in your life that you're presented with an option that just might be for the greater good.'

Then she smiled up at Walter, who was clearing the plates from the main course. 'Do your puddings match your mains?'

'They certainly do, miss,' Walter said, and he beamed.

'I'd like something rich and sticky.'

'I believe we can accommodate that, miss.' Walter was smiling down at her like an avuncular genie. It was as if she had him mesmerised. Well, why not? Nick thought. He was feeling pretty mesmerised himself.

'Pudding for you, too?' Walter said, beaming still, and Nick nodded before thinking about it.

What was he doing? He seldom had pudding. He had to get his mind back into gear. Now.

'I don't know the first thing about you,' he said weakly to Rose as Walter headed off to fetch puddings for all. 'How can we think about marriage?'

'Are you worried?' she asked. 'I'm not an axe murderer. Nor a husband beater. Are you?'

He ignored the question. 'Erhard says you're widowed.'

'Yes,' she said in a voice that suddenly said 'don't go there'.

'There's no impediment to marriage,' Erhard said, stepping into the breach.

'Except that I don't much want to be married,' he said. Or he didn't think he did. He *hadn't* thought he did. There seemed to be two strands of thought here. The strand that he'd had before meeting Rose, and the post-Rose strand. Actually the 'post-Rose' was a really convoluted knot.

'Neither do I,' said Rose. 'Isn't that lucky? We wouldn't need to stay married, would we, Erhard?'

'Of course not,' Erhard said. 'This isn't a happy-ever-after scenario I'm demanding of you. The idea is that you marry almost immediately. I'll put the necessary paperwork in train, and then we present you to Alp de Montez as the Jacques-Julianna alternative. I've had private words with the committee. Nick, you stay in Alp de Montez for a few weeks, until things seem settled. Maybe a month. Then you use the excuse that you don't want to give up your profession and return to London. Rose then stays in Alp de Montez until we can get things in train to get a decent government sorted. When affairs are under control, you can quietly divorce.'

'You'd depend on Rose to get the affairs under control?'

'You're the international lawyer,' Erhard said shrewdly. 'I'm willing to wager you know exactly what can be done.'

He did. He'd been thinking about it all week. The chance to make a difference….

He'd never belonged. His mother, Zia, had left Alp de Montez as a troubled teenager. She'd ended up in Australia, addicted to drugs, pregnant with him. His childhood until he was eight had been a struggle to survive, lurching from fleeting intervals living with his increasingly erratic mother, to extended periods in a long string of foster homes.

Then Ruby had found him. She'd plucked him off the streets of Sydney, and from then on his base had been with Ruby and her tribe of foster sons. Ruby had given him security, but still he felt rootless.

At some really basic level Erhard's proposition left him breathless. What had Rose said? An option 'for the greater good'. It just might be the chance to make a difference.

He thought back to the frightened girl who'd been his mother. She'd want this. He knew she would. She'd been desperately homesick for Alp de Montez but there was no way her increasingly disgusted family would have funded her to go home.

He could go home on her behalf now. With this woman by his side.

Marriage. It wasn't such a frightening thought if it was done for the right reasons. But were Rose's reasons right? How could a woman like this want to marry a complete stranger?

She was his cousin.

No. She wasn't even that, he thought. She was the product of his aunt-by-marriage's affair with someone they knew nothing of.

It didn't matter. She was gorgeous.

'What about Julianna?' he asked, looking for catches. 'You can't convince her to do the right thing?'

'Julianna won't speak to me,' Erhard said.

'But you?' he asked Rose. 'You're her sister.'

'She doesn't speak to me either,' Rose said sadly. 'I know it's dumb, but there it is.'

'So this really is a serious proposition.'

'It seems like it.' She smiled ruefully into her empty wine-glass. 'You know, I swore I'd never marry again.'

'That'd be a waste.'

'Says you, who's never married at all,' she retorted, suddenly sounding angry.

'I'm sorry.' But his thoughts were elsewhere. 'I wouldn't need to stay in Alp de Montez,' he said slowly.

'You would for a few weeks,' Erhard said. 'Could you use a holiday?'

A holiday. Strange concept. With Rose?

She really was the most extraordinary woman. Stunning.

'Maybe I could,' he said. 'And you?' he queried Rose. 'How long would you have to be away from your vet practice?'

'A year,' Erhard said, answering for her. 'At least. Maybe longer. I'm sorry, Rose, but it'd be more your commitment than Nick's. You'd rule jointly, but it's you who's first in line. Unless anything happened to Julianna…'

'Which isn't going to happen,' Rose said, and shivered. And then braced herself. 'No matter. I'd have to close my doors anyway, and there are…reasons why that's not such a terrible idea.'

'I guess the idea of playing princess for a year would be fun,' Nick ventured, and she frowned.

'Now you're being insulting,' she retorted, and he paused.

Maybe he was.

There's not so many times in your life that you're presented with an option that just might be for the greater good.

She met his look with calm indifference, almost

scorn. His gaze fell to her hands. Here was another difference—a huge difference—from the women he dated. This woman's hands wouldn't have looked out of place on a woman twenty years older. Work-worn hands, not something he saw a lot of.

But she was looking down at his hands, and he suddenly realised she knew exactly what he was thinking. His hands were those of an international lawyer. There was not a lot of work wear there.

If she was to have fun for a year, maybe there were reasons she deserved it, he thought. She'd lost a husband…

On the far side of the restaurant, a band struck up. It was a simple quartet, playing softly enough to not disturb the diners on this side of the restaurant. There was a small dance-floor, and a couple of diners rose and started dancing.

To Nick's surprise Erhard rose. But not to dance.

'No,' he said as Nick rose as well. 'I'm sorry.' He sighed. 'I'm not…completely well. If you'll excuse me for a moment…' He looked across at the dance floor, almost wistfully. 'Maybe you could dance while I'm away.'

'I don't—' Nick started, but Erhard shook his head.

'You do. My informants say you do. And so does Rose.' He gave an uncertain smile at them both, but there was discomfort behind his eyes.

'Excuse me. You go on.' And he pressed his napkin to his lips and headed towards the rear of the restaurant.

Rose watched him go in concern. 'He seems a nice man,' she said. 'He's ill. I wonder what—'

'He's probably doing this to manipulate us,' Nick retorted, and she smiled, but absently, still looking concerned.

'I don't think so. Even if he is, he's doing it for the right reasons, and there is something wrong. I think.'

The silence stretched on. Behind them the band launched into a lively Latin-swing number.

Nick was already standing. He went to sit down again but then thought it seemed surly.

The woman before him was beautiful.

'You don't look like a country vet,' he said, and he must have sounded accusing because she smiled again.

'I'm not manipulating,' she said gently. 'I promise.'

But any woman who looked like she did tonight was making a statement, he thought, whether it was manipulative or not. And maybe his thoughts were transparent, because her smile gave way to a flash of anger.

'Stop looking like that. I have the right to wear what I like.'

'Of course you do.'

'My husband bought this for me on our honeymoon,' she said, still angry, and he stilled.

'So it is a sort of statement.'

'I guess it is.'

'A statement that you're available?'

The flash of anger stilled and her eyes were suddenly ice. 'I don't think I want to be married to you,' she snapped. 'Of all the boorish comments… If you wear a nice suit, is that an advertisement of availability as well?'

'No,' he said, horrified. He was suddenly way out of his depth. How could he have asked her such a question? As well as being insulting, he'd also hurt her. He could see it in the way she'd withdrawn.

'Rose, I'm sorry,' he said. 'I have no idea why I said that, but it was way out of line. Hell, marriage or not, we seem to have crossed some sort of barrier that's launched me somewhere where I'm not sure of the rules any more. I know that's no excuse. But please—I'm sorry.'

Her face softened—just a little. 'It does seem crazy,' she admitted. She glanced down at her dress ruefully. 'But maybe this is some sort of a statement. Maybe that's why you've made me angry. You know, this dress has sat in a camphor chest in my parents-in-law's house for the last five years. It's been like…well, I was locked up with it. Tonight I did wear it as a kind of declaration— not that I'm available, but that I'm free. If that makes sense.' She shook her head. 'No. It barely makes sense to me. But the last thing I want is more attachments. I've done family for life. I *am* free.'

'Diving into the royal goldfish bowl of Alp de Montez is scarcely freeing yourself,' he said cautiously.

'It all depends on what your prison has been,' she said. 'Are you going to ask me to dance?'

'I…' What the hell? 'Yes.'

'Excellent,' she said, and she smiled, rose and took his arm, altogether proprietary. It seemed as if he was forgiven. 'If I'm going to get the camphor smell out of this dress then I need to swirl it round a bit.'

She didn't smell of camphor.

Rose was an intuitive dancer, light and lovely on her feet. Nick had been taught the rudiments of dance by his determined little foster mother, and he'd always enjoyed it. With great music and a good partner one could almost lose oneself in dance.

But not tonight. He didn't want to lose himself when he was dancing with Rose.

The Latin music gave way to a gentle waltz. Erhard had still not returned to their table so suddenly Nick was holding her close, steering her around the dance floor, feeling her body mould to his in perfect time with his steps, in perfect time with him.

And she didn't smell of camphor. She smelled of Rose.

What was she doing? She'd brought this dress with her on a whim, walking out of the house feeling as if she'd betrayed everyone. She hadn't been worried about what she was wearing. But as her mother-in-law's weeping had increased, as her father-in-law had wrung his hands and said, 'Rose, you can't leave. We love you. You're our daughter. What would Max think?' she'd abandoned her distress as too hard and she'd let anger hold sway.

She'd lifted the lid of her camphor chest and had retrieved the dress and shoes that had lain there for what seemed almost a lifetime.

And then, before she'd closed the chest again, she'd taken Max's photograph from her bedside table and put it where her dress had been.

And had closed the lid.

Then she'd walked out of the house. Free.

No, not free. Still guilt-ridden. Seemingly obligated in some weird way to a country she'd left with the royal family's scorn following her.

But she wasn't going back to Yorkshire except to finalise things. No family. No ties. Nick's question as to her availability couldn't have been

more wrong. If ever anyone else told her they
loved her then she'd run a mile.

But she was in this man's arms.

Yes, and that was great, she told herself as she
let him swirl her round the dance floor with an ex-
pertise that made her feel wonderful. Erhard's long
letter had filled her in on who Nick was. A loner
who'd pulled himself up the hard way. A man
whose intelligence was extraordinary. A man with
an Aussie accent overlaying his smooth French-
Italian native tongue, and a laid-back charm that
could knock a girl sideways. Nick was a sophisticated international lawyer who'd come from a
background even more dysfunctional than her own.

He was a man who knew where his bound-
aries were.

So it was fine. Yes, she could marry him to
keep Alp de Montez safe, and she could keep her
independence. It would finally make her free.

Please.

Five minutes later Erhard returned to the table.
The musicians took a break. There was no reason
to stay on the dance floor, but as Nick led her back
to the table he was aware of a sharp stab of regret.

Only because he loved dancing, he thought.
Only that.

Erhard was smiling, watching them weave their

way through the tables to join him. The strain
had eased from his face a little.

'Two wonderful dancers,' he said softly as they
sat down again. 'You see, this thing becomes
possible.' He settled back into his chair and took
a long sip of water. 'Well?'

Nick looked at Rose and found she was
watching him. Intently.

It seemed a decision needed to be made. Now.
Did that mean Rose had already decided?

'You need to trust me,' Erhard told him softly.
'This is a big ask. We need to trust each other.'

'It's fine,' Rose said, suddenly sounding impa-
tient to move on. Sounding as if she was annoyed.
'I'm willing to take a chance, so it's up to you,
Nick. If you don't choose to take part, then say
so now. Let Erhard go into damage control and
see if there's another solution.'

'There's no other solution,' Erhard said flatly,
and they both went back to watching him.

She'd flung her hat in the ring, just like that.
She'd agreed to marry him after knowing him
only a matter of hours.

His foundations were shaken, he thought, and
it wasn't just this crazy proposition that was
shaking them. It was the way he'd felt, dancing
with Rose. The way she'd felt...

He needed a cold shower, and then some good
legal advice.

'You're holding a gun to my head,' he snapped, and the old man shook his head.

'That's what we're hoping to avoid. Guns.'

'You're serious?'

'I'm serious,' Erhard whispered, and the grey look flooded back. How ill was he?

'So tell us,' Rose said to Nick directly, with a sideways glance of concern towards Erhard. 'Are you in or are you out?'

'I need to do a little more research…'

'Fine,' she said. 'Research away. I spent a week on the internet myself. But if you come up with the conclusion I came up with—as you will—are you ready to have a go at fixing things?'

'You're seriously asking me to marry you?'

'I thought you were asking me to marry you.'

'I guess it's mutual.'

'Only I've said yes, and you haven't,' she said. 'Go on. It might even be fun.'

'I don't do fun.'

'Neither do I,' she snapped. 'Not for years. So we're perfectly compatible. I'm willing to take a risk on the rest. What about you? Yes or no?'

And there it was. Not a gun pointing at his head, but just possibly a chance to make a difference.

Rose was waiting for him to come to a decision, her grey eyes calmly watchful.

Erhard was waiting too. Two people he instinctively trusted who were trying to do good.

So what was a man to say?

'Yes,' he said, and there was a moment's stunned silence, and then they both beamed.

'There it is, then,' Rose said. 'Proposal accepted. Congratulations to us all, and here comes pudding. Do you think I might have some more champagne?'

CHAPTER THREE

ROSE finished an excellent pudding, but it signalled that the night, for Rose at least, was over. She excused herself without waiting for coffee.

'I was up before dawn, and I need to walk a bit before bed after all that champagne,' she told them. 'No, I don't want company. I need head-space to plan the next few weeks. There's so much I need to do. Finding someone to take care of a thousand square-miles of farm animals is the least of it.'

'If there are no hitches then you can marry in four weeks,' Erhard said. 'Marrying in Alp de Montez is the wisest course. Can you be ready then?'

'I'll do my best,' Rose said. She hesitated, and then she stooped and kissed the old man gently on the forehead. 'You take care of yourself. Please. For me.'

And she left without another word.

Nick watched as she wove through the tables, smiling as a waiter paused to let her pass, smiling at the doorman as he opened the door for her, smiling as she went out into the night.

'She's some lady,' Erhard said gently, and Nick came back to earth with a jolt.

'Sorry. I was just thinking.'

'She's worth thinking about.'

'I don't…'

'No, you don't, do you?' Erhard said. 'I've had you thoroughly checked. The longest you've ever dated one woman is nine weeks.'

That took him aback. 'You know that?'

'The investigative agency I hired is very thorough.'

'So you know all about me.'

'It wouldn't have been worth my while to approach you if I'd found you were another Jacques. But the reputation you have in legal circles is for integrity. You try to select cases where there's moral imperative, as well as financial. Also, the woman who fostered you since you were small— Ruby—says that you're honest, kind and trust-worthy. As a reference I thought that was the best.'

'How the hell did you get Ruby to talk about me?' he demanded, and Erhard gave a small smile.

'The investigative agency has an operative who enjoys macramé,' he confessed. 'She infiltrated your foster mother's macramé group.' His smile broadened at Nick's astonishment. 'Desperate times call for desperate measures. Ruby seemed to be the best person to give a character reference, but she'd never have answered an official request with such honesty.

'As it was, she told our operative that you went through eight foster homes as your mother agonised whether she could keep you. That you grieved for your mother, even though she was…impossible. That once you joined Ruby and her family of foster sons you were fiercely loyal to every one of the family members. That you learned early to be a loner, but you were generous to a fault. There's an Australian children's home—Castle, at Dolphin Bay?—that you contribute to in any way you can. That if any of your foster brothers are in trouble you're there before they ask.' His smile deepened. 'I read the report and I thought, yes, you'll do.'

'Ruby's macramé group.' He was still feeling winded. Rose was out the door now, and the room was dreary for her going. Well, then. Erhard and his 'operatives' had to be good for something. 'Rose?' he queried. 'What did you find out about Rose?'

'I've told you most of it.'

'Tell me again,' he growled. He hadn't listened properly the first time. He hadn't been as interested as he was now.

'She's had it hard too,' Erhard said gently, with only a faint smile to tell he'd guessed at Nick's reactions. 'Maybe almost as hard as you. Her mother had rheumatoid arthritis and couldn't work, and after she left the palace Eric simply ignored both of them. Rose worked her way through vet school. She met and married a fellow student—Max McCray. Max was an older student—he'd missed schooling because of time spent recovering from cancer. Max was the only son of a veterinarian in the Yorkshire Dales. Rose was embraced into Max's family, and when Rose and Max graduated they took over the family veterinary practice. Then the disease recurred. Rose cared for Max devotedly—as well as running the vet practice—until Max's death two years ago. She's running it still.'

'But she's agreed to leave.'

'You know, I suspect there's almost an element of relief,' Erhard said honestly. 'The village she's been living in is tiny, and she's very much Max's widow. Everywhere we asked we were told how wonderful Rose is, and how noble it is of her to carry on her husband's work. There's a large veterinary conglomerate based in a nearby town that would buy them out in a flash, but her parents-in-law won't hear of it. So she's stuck dealing with lots of farm work—horses and cattle—which her father-in-law and husband loved, but it's hard physical work for one so slight. There's also been a huge money problem.

Max's illness put her in debt, and she'd borrowed to put herself through vet school. Max had no family money.'

'You know…' He hesitated. 'This isn't a standard private-investigative report, but the firm I use is good—very good. Their brief is to compile character assessments of people in line for top jobs, so they give more than facts. Our investigator talked to one of the nurses who cared for Rose's husband. The nurse's assessment is that Rose is stuck in her husband's life.'

'But she *is* leaving.'

'We've given her a huge moral imperative to leave,' Erhard said. 'A whole country depending on her instead of just a village. She can walk away without Max's ghost dragging her back.'

'So you're expecting me to walk away from my profession like you're expecting Rose to?'

'No one's expecting anything of you,' Erhard said patiently. 'Apart from a few weeks of your time and a name on a marriage document. There's no need for you to stay in Alp de Montez. There's no need for your life to change very much at all. Simply take a few weeks off work, marry Rose, wait until the fuss about the succession has died down and then take over your life again. Yes, you'll be part of the royal couple, but apart from the coronation itself—and the wedding—your attendance is optional. Your interest is optional, and when

Rose's position is established you can divorce.
Rose seems willing to put in the hard yards.'

'You said she's working too hard as it is,' Nick
said, frowning.

'I'll take care of her,' Erhard said. 'She won't
be delivering calves in icy paddocks at midnight.'

'That's what she's doing now?'

'That's what she's doing. Living with her parents-
in-law. Stuck in the grief of her husband's loss.'

There were so many facets of the woman, he
thought. A cheeky imp. A beautiful, sophisticated
woman. A magical dancer. A workhorse.

'I guess I can,' he said, and Erhard smiled.

'There are worse women to marry than Rose,'
he said.

It seemed the thing was decided. By the time he
turned up at work the next morning, Erhard had
already initiated the first steps towards the royal
wedding. Nick took a deep breath and quietly
talked to the firm's senior partners. To his relief,
the partners saw nothing but benefit. Even Blake,
Nick's foster brother who also worked for the
firm, was enthusiastic.

When Nick told him, Blake stared at his foster
brother in amazement, and then quietly gone away
and done the same research Nick had. Even to
Blake the plan looked solid. 'It's your birthright,
after all, and you'd be crazy not to,' Blake told him.

'There's enough stability in the country for your marriage to be received with relief. You get in there and support Rose-Anitra for all you're worth.'

'But marriage…' he said to Blake, and Blake grinned.

'Yeah, well, maybe this is the only sort of marriage that can work for the likes of us,' he'd said. 'It's not like you want a real marriage. Why not in name only?'

Why not? *Because it wasn't quite true.*

Marriage, for Nick, had always seemed something others did. From the time he first remembered, it had been as if he was on the outside looking in. Happy families? How did you go about achieving that? He had six foster brothers and they'd all come from disasters—partnerships that had imploded. Even Ruby, his beloved foster mother, had suffered tragedy.

He'd dated many women—of course he had—but the step toward commitment had always seemed insurmountable. But this…

'You're only committing for a month, right?' Blake asked.

'The general idea is that we stay married for as long as we need to. Minimum a month. Once Rose is firmly entrenched, there's no need for me to stay.'

'But the thought of helping get the country on its feet again turns you on?'

'It does, yeah,' he admitted.

'And the thought of being married to Rose?'

He grinned and didn't answer. But the bubble of excitement was becoming a tidal wave. This was a challenge. It was potentially beneficial for a whole country. And he'd be marrying Rose. If it worked out...

See, *there* was the scary bit. For some dumb reason, that was the thing that gave him pause. The way he felt about her.

She was gorgeous. Her smile made him gasp. She felt...

She didn't feel anything. What had she said? 'The last thing I want is more attachments. I've done family for life. I am free'.

That should make him feel better about the whole deal. Instead, it only made him feel more uncertain.

The thought of taking on a country's direction didn't worry him. The thought of marrying Rose did. Or, it didn't worry him as much as unsettle him. It made him feel like he was teetering on the edge of something he didn't understand.

But Blake didn't see that. No one did. He himself decided it was dumb, and as a week passed without seeing Rose he thought, okay, he was being a romantic fool. This was hardly a romantic wedding. It seemed more like a military operation, and he had to treat it as such.

Erhard was on the phone constantly, organising every tiny detail—when they'd arrive, when the wedding would take place, accommodation, transport, meetings with the council to take place as soon as the wedding was over, the ascendancy claim. The legal documents Erhard faxed for signature made even Nick's eyes water.

What was Rose thinking? But he couldn't know.

'I have a mountain of organisation to get through before I leave,' she'd told him in their one brief phone-call. 'I'm dealing with mass hysteria here. You sort the legal stuff. I know it's dumb, but I'll sign whatever needs to be signed. I have to trust you on this, Nick. You and Erhard.'

A later phone call elicited a bit more background. Instead of Rose, his call was answered by her mother-in-law.

'You have no right to do this,' the woman hissed down the phone. 'The whole town depends on her. She's saying the district will have to join the vet co-operative in the next town. She says with the money they pay we'll be well off, but we don't want money. My poor son would turn in his grave. How dare that man tell her she has no choice? How dare…?'

She became almost venomous, and in the end Nick had put down the phone, and thought he could understand another of Rose's conditions. She didn't want any press release until she was out of the country.

Erhard agreed with that reluctantly, but Nick thought that was fine. The juggernaut that was royal ascension rolled on.

Then, in the last few days before he and Rose were due to fly out, Nick's contact with Erhard had faltered. There was one stilted phone-call. 'Nikolai, things are in place for you to take over. I need to fade into the background. Good luck to you and to Rose.'

He didn't explain, but by the sound of his voice Nick thought that his health was probably a factor. Erhard had launched them, and was depending on them to take it from here.

Good luck to you and to Rose.

That caused another of those moments when panic seemed to overwhelm him. But there was no reason for panic. No logical reason.

A royal marriage of convenience. Why not?

So he went on planning for this strange wedding, and the world didn't crash on his head.

But on that last day, when he walked out of his office before taking a month off, and he found the whole of the office decorated with bridal nonsense, he was forced to see this for the reality it was. It was Saturday. The office should have been deserted, but people had obviously come in especially. Obviously Blake and the partners had decided that today they'd break their silence. Champagne was flowing. The girls from the typing pool were handing round wedding-cake.

Blake had found a picture of Rose in a local newspaper's weddings column, detailing Rose's wedding to Max years ago. Someone had blown her image up to banner size. Posters of a grainy, bridal Rose were plastered from one end of the office to another.

'She's gorgeous,' everyone agreed, and even Rose, laughing down from every wall, seemed to concur.

Rose's image unsettled him as nothing else could. This was a Rose without the care lines around her eyes. Rose before…life?

It felt weird that he could think of marrying this woman, he decided, trying to smile as he accepted congratulations. It even seemed dangerous. But he'd gone too far to back out now, and finally he escaped, under a shower of confetti and good-natured banter.

'There goes the groom to collect his bride. Or the prince to collect his princess,' they called after him, and he had to smile and concur.

'You'll be the second of Ruby's foster sons to get leg-shackled,' Blake said as he walked with his foster brother to the firm's car-park. He and Blake had gone through a lot together. They'd come from similar dysfunctional backgrounds, ending up under Ruby's care. They'd both been ambitious, and they'd made it through law school together. Nick had started work with this firm first, and Blake had followed the year after. They were about as close as brothers could be, which gave Blake the right to say what he liked. Which he intended to do right now.

'You're not looking happy,' he said thoughtfully. 'Bridal jitters getting to you?'

'You know this isn't a real wedding,' Nick growled, unnerved, but Blake smiled and shrugged.

'You make the vows. It's all the wedding the likes of us can do. What have you told Ruby?'

'That I've agreed to be married for a month in order for Rose to ascend the throne. That it's business only. That she needn't worry about anything, and I'll come over and pay her a visit when it's all over.

'And she said?' Blake said cautiously.

'She…um…sounded a little irate. I thought she might have phoned you.'

'When did you tell her?'

'This morning.'

'You have to be kidding.' He and Blake were pushing their way through a crowd of photographers on the pavement. The press had arrived seemingly out of nowhere. Someone must have told them what was happening, and they were now documenting every step. 'She'll probably have tried to phone me twenty times already.'

'Just assure her it's business,' Nick said. 'She shouldn't worry about it. It's nothing.'

'Nothing.' Blake stopped dead, his face a picture of incredulity. 'You want me to explain to Ruby you're marrying a princess but it's *nothing*? I'd be lucky to get off with burst eardrums.'

'Then don't. Ruby's agreed to do some baby-sitting for Pierce and his brood for a couple of weeks, so she won't have time to think about it.'

'They do have news services in Dolphin Bay,' Blake said with asperity. 'Australia's not so far away as you'd think when it comes to royal weddings. I seem to remember they even have newspapers. You're inviting guests to this wedding?'

'Only dignitaries. You can tell Ruby that.' He gave a rueful grin. 'I tried, but she wouldn't stop yelling.'

'You're seriously getting married without involving family?'

'I don't do family. You know that.'

'Yeah, but does Ruby? She'll be over here like a flash, taking Rose into the bosom of our peculiar family, finding out her sweater size, making a macramé spread for the marital bed, maybe even starting on a few booties.'

'See, that's what we don't want,' Nick said bluntly. 'If I let Ruby near Rose, Rose would run like a scalded cat. This is business.'

'A marriage made in heaven,' Blake said wryly.

'It's the only sort Rose will consider,' Nick told him, and didn't notice when Blake gave him an odd look. They'd reached his car now. The photographers were still at it. Somehow they had to be ignored.

Problems needed to be ignored. Meanwhile he gripped his brother's hand in a gesture of farewell. 'Thanks, mate,' he told him. 'Keep my place here warm for me.'

'You might not still want it,' Blake said, still looking at him strangely.

'Of course I will. This marriage is for a matter of weeks. That's all it's for. I'll be back.'

'Yeah,' Blake said and shook his hand back. 'Right. Just you be careful boyo, of marital threads as well as political ones.'

So what was the problem? Why did Blake sound dubious?

And where had those photographers come from? Surely they wouldn't spread this news as far as Ruby in Dolphin Bay?

Maybe he should have given Ruby a few more details. Maybe even invited her to the wedding.

But Ruby at his wedding? She'd sob, he thought. She'd hug them both. She'd make it incredibly, intensely personal.

Which would scare Rose.

And him.

In the comparative privacy of his BMW, heading for his Kensington apartment to collect his baggage, Nick had time to think, and the more he thought the more he felt like he was heading into trouble. To hurt Ruby by not inviting her…

He couldn't invite her. And he'd specified it was just business.

But it had his foot easing from the accelerator, thinking maybe even now it wasn't too late to draw back.

His mobile phone rang. It answered automatically on the hands-free base. If it hadn't, maybe he wouldn't have answered. His need for solitude to get his head right was starting to be overwhelming. But the voice came on the other end of the line before he could prevent the connection. 'Nick?'

'Rose.' She sounded as spooked as he was. 'It's good to hear from you,' he managed.

'There are photographers here,' she said. 'Everywhere. They arrived an hour ago and there's more arriving by the minute. My mother-in-law's weeping so hard she's making herself ill. The phone's ringing off the hook. I think…is this a disaster?'

So he wasn't alone in feeling overwhelmed. 'I guess it's what we had to expect,' he said cautiously, insensibly reassured that she was feeling the same as he was.

'I hadn't thought…'

'Neither had I.'

'It's not too late to back out,' she whispered.

'Do you want to back out?'

'I don't know,' she said. 'It seemed so easy when it was just fantasy. But now…'

'What would you do if you backed out?' he asked.

There was a long silence. 'Stay here, I guess,' she said, sounding unsure.

'You don't want to stay there?'

'No.' That was unequivocal, at any rate. Then, 'We did decide to do this for the right reasons, didn't we, Nick?'

He had to be honest here. 'Yes.'

'It will make life better for the people of Alp de Montez?'

'I think so,' he said reluctantly. 'My law firm is heavily geared to international disputes. We have people on the ground all over the world. The consensus is that we really can make a difference.'

'We don't have a choice then,' she said heavily.

'There is a choice, Rose,' he said. He'd pulled up at traffic lights. They'd turned green, but he wasn't shifting. There were horns blaring behind him but he thought, no, he had to concentrate. 'You can walk away.'

'I can't walk away,' she said. 'Unless I have an alternative.'

'You can stay where you are.'

'That's what I meant,' she whispered. 'Alp de Montez is my alternative.'

He didn't understand. 'Look, we can call the whole thing off.'

'Do you want to?'

'Hold on a minute,' he told her, and moved forward before the motorists banked up behind him got out of their cars and thumped him. He steered into a bus stop and stopped. 'Rose, this is up to you,' he said gently. 'You're the one first in line. I'm the supporting role here.'

'I guess.' She took a ragged breath. 'But you will support me?'

Five minutes ago he'd been thinking he couldn't. But now… It was only for a month or so, and it would make a difference. Rose was taking this on for much, much longer.

If she was prepared to do it, how could he say no?

'Of course I'll support you,' he said gently. 'We're in this together.'

'For a month.'

'And then I'll be on the end of the phone. I won't leave you isolated. We'll set up supports.'

'But you'll stay involved?'

He took a deep breath. 'Yes.' Where had that come from? The Nikolai de Montez mantra was 'never get involved'. But this was different. This was for a country.

This was for Rose.

'Yes,' he said again. 'I'll stay as involved as you want.'

'Then I guess I can cope with the press,' she said, still sounding shaky. 'The plane's due to pick me up in Newcastle at two. You swear you'll be on it?'

What was a man to say to that? Despite misgivings. Despite Ruby.

'Yes,' he said, and he was committed.

CHAPTER FOUR

THE plane was fitted out like something out of a James Bond movie. Nikolai was accustomed to first-class international travel, but this was mind boggling.

He couldn't cut and run now, leaving Rose to face the consequences, but he felt like it. He buckled his seat belt with grim resolution. *Let's get this over with.*

For the first part of the flight he was alone, apart from a dark-suited, elderly attendant who spoke in monosyllables. Somewhere up front there'd be a flight crew, but he never saw them. Erhard had made the arrangements. He just had to trust Erhard. Only, why hadn't Erhard answered his calls for the last few days? How sick was he?

What was Nick walking into?

Rose was due to catch the flight in Newcastle. He'd committed. To marriage.

Yes, to marriage, and it seemed weird. He

sank into the luxurious upholstery and let his thoughts go where they willed. They asked questions he couldn't answer. Things like, would Rose get cold feet? What if Erhard's illness wasn't the reason for his withdrawal? How alone would they be?

It wasn't an uncivilised country they were going to, he told himself, his unease deepening with every mile they drew further from London. The worst that could happen was that he and Rose were asked to leave. Or refused permission to land.

The plane was in the air. His escape was cut off. Next step Rose.

'Would you like refreshments? A beer?' an expressionless fight attendant—Griswold, according to his name badge—asked him, and Nick shook his head.

'No, thank you.' He didn't need a beer. He needed to keep every faculty crystal-clear.

The attendant, a sober-suited man in his sixties, gave him a searching look. Nick smiled; the man seemed anxious and the last thing Nick wanted to do was make the locals nervous. But Griswold simply bowed briefly and left him alone.

And then they were landing at Newcastle. Griswold appeared again and told him there was no need for him to stir. 'The Princess Rose-Anitra is in the terminal,' he told him. 'It's raining outside. I'd advise you to stay put.'

The Princess Rose-Anitra. The name took him aback.

The Princess Rose-Anitra, boarding the official plane of the royal family of Alp de Montez. To join her future husband.

The fantasy had begun.

And here came the bride. Right—*not*. This wasn't your normal vision of a royal bride. Rose was running across the rain-soaked tarmac. An airport official was holding an umbrella over her head, trying to keep up with her. She was dressed in jeans and an ancient duffel coat. She was carrying a shabby holdall.

She was also carrying a dog. Some sort of terrier.

His feeling of unreality took a step back. Rose grounded this thing in practicality, he thought, and the craziness seemed possible again as he watched her run.

Seemingly ignoring the rain, she smiled at Griswold at the foot of the stairs, and Nick found himself smiling back. This wasn't fantasy. Rose was a country veterinarian with a scruffy looking dog and clothes past their use-by date.

She just looked like…Rose.

She stepped into the cabin, laughing at something Griswold said behind her, speaking in a language Nick recognised.

She saw him and she stopped short. Her smile

faded, and she looked suddenly uncertain. Maybe even a little scared.

'Um… Hi,' she said.

'Hi.' As a response to the occasion it lacked a certain sophistication, but for the life of him he couldn't think of a more intelligent response.

'You don't mind sharing a cabin with Hoppy?' she asked.

'Hoppy?'

'Because of the leg,' she said kindly, as if he was a bit thick. She smiled down at the little dog in her arms and then checked out the plane. She seemed almost overwhelmed by its opulence, swallowing a couple of times like she was trying to dredge up courage. But somehow she made her voice light and smiley. 'Wow,' she whispered. 'I've hardly ever flown before. Surely they can't all be like this?'

'No,' Nick said. They certainly weren't. The two double settees that were the airline's only passenger seats were more luxurious than any seat he'd ever been in. They were fitted with seat belts, but that was their only concession to airline strictures. There was white shag-pile carpet. There were tiny side-tables with indents to hold wine glasses—all carved from the one magnificent piece of mahogany. A partition at the rear led to a bedroom—he could see a magnificent bed set up, ready for use. The entire interior was painted white with muted pinks, with soft hangings disguising the harsh outer casing of the airline's metal cabin.

This was definitely not cattle class.

But Rose had moved on, shrugging off her discomfort with her coat. She placed the little dog on the seat beside him. Griswold—who'd spoken hardly at all since Nick had come aboard—took her coat and smiled down at Hoppy.

'*Le chien a faim? Peut-être il voudrait un petit morceau de biftek?*'

'Hoppy would very much like a *biftek*,' Rose said, and beamed at the man. '*Moi aussi. Oui. Merci beaucoup.*'

'*Et pour la madame, du champagne?*'

'Ooh, yes. *Oui. Merci, merci, merci.*' She lifted her dog back into her arms, sank down into the seat beside Nick and giggled. 'Isn't this fabulous?'

The dog only had three legs. Hoppy. Yep, he had it. He was right on the ball today. If only she didn't smile so much.

'Do you suppose there'd be caviar if I asked for it?' she said, and he decided to stop the fatuousness and try and be serious.

'I thought the plan was to stop extravagant spending by the royal family.'

'Oh,' she said, and her face fell. 'Does that have to start today? I thought maybe we could have a little bit of fun first.' Her laughter disappeared as if he'd reprimanded her. She sank back into the sumptuous upholstery, clipped her seat belt and hugged her dog.

He felt bad. He hadn't meant to stop her smiling.

She stayed looking defensive. He went on feeling bad. And more.

More? Yes, more. Because suddenly he was hit with this really dumb urge to kiss her better.

Or just to kiss her.

Which was really dumb, he told himself, startled by the intensity of his urge as well as the unexpectedness of it. That would be really stupid.

As was her reaction, he thought, struggling for an even keel. She was acting like he'd slapped her. He was starting to feel like he was always apologising to this woman. She made him feel he was permanently on the back foot.

But if he was going to apologise he might as well get it over with.

'Maybe I was out of order,' he conceded. 'I'm sorry.'

'There's a concession,' she said. 'But of course you're right. This is a serious business. A marriage of convenience. There's not a lot to smile about in that.'

They didn't speak again as the plane took off. The two settees-cum-airline-seats were forward facing, set in a V, so up to four occupants could talk together. There was a silk-hung divider in front which hid the service compartment and the entrance to the cockpit, but they were essentially alone.

They were sitting side by side, and he felt… weird. She was very close.

But not for long. The plane rose smoothly and the seat-belt sign clicked off. The moment it did Rose gathered Hoppy, unclipped her seat belt and moved herself sharply across the aisle to the other double seat. To the furthest side of the far seat.

It was like she'd slapped him. Even Hoppy was looking balefully across at him, like he'd offended the dog too.

'I have offended you,' he said, frowning, and she shook her head.

'No. I just decided you're right. It's formal, the stuff we'll be doing, so I may as well start being formal now.'

'You could have caviar if you want. If it's aboard.'

'I don't really want it.'

'But you asked…'

'I just thought maybe it'd be fun to play the princess a little,' she said, and then looked ruefully down at her faded jeans and her three-legged dog. 'But I'm not princess material. I never have been.'

'Cinderella before the godmother?'

'Yeah, well, the godmother's the money thing,' she said. 'Bane of my life.' Griswold came through, bearing a tray carrying one crystal flute, the champagne bubbling deliciously. She looked at the champagne with regret.

'Do you think I should ask for it to be put back in the bottle?'

'I don't think it can be,' he said weakly. Hell, how to make a man feel bad...

'You mean I just have to drink it?' She cheered up. 'To save its life? Hooray.' Griswold smiled as she buried her nose in bubbles. 'Are you having one?'

'I'll have a glass of wine with my meal.'

She raised her eyebrows. 'And more than one never touches your lips?'

'I believe it'd be good if at least one of us kept our wits about us.' *Um...* He hadn't meant to say that. It was just that she made him feel *old*. No. Defensive, he decided, but he didn't know why.

And she seemed to agree with him.

'Of course,' she said, and raised her glass in his direction. 'How very wise. You stay on watch. You keep all your wits while I stick my nose into champagne.'

Why had he said that?

He sounded about a hundred. Talk about a killjoy...

He thought of what Erhard had told him about this woman. She'd had it tough for the past few years. No wonder she'd been talked into accepting her heritage. No wonder she wanted to escape to a little fantasy.

He glanced across to the other seat. In between sipping champagne she was hugging her little dog to her like a shield. She looked about ten years old.

'I'm really sorry I was mean,' he said, and she flashed him a suspicious look.

'Lawyers don't apologise. If you acknowledge fault, then I get to sue.'

So maybe she wasn't ten years old.

'Tell me about your dog.'

'He's Hoppy.'

'We've done that. I was hoping for a little more information.'

She looked at him suspiciously over the rim of her champagne glass.

'Hoppy's two years old,' she said at last. 'He got squashed by a tractor when he was five weeks old. I was helping deliver a foal, and the farmer was driving his tractor through the yard. Mud everywhere. This little one darted out to meet me, and went straight under the tractor wheel. When the tractor moved on we couldn't see a sign of him. Then thirty seconds later I found him buried completely in mud. One leg was broken so badly it had to come off, but otherwise he was perfect. He even wiggled his tail when I patted him, smashed leg and all.'

'So you bought him?'

'I was given him. The farmer's reaction to the accident was that it was a shame he hadn't been killed outright. Hoppy's so small he's useless for ratting. That's why he'd been bred. So I have my semi-useless, non-ratting Hoppy, and I love him to bits.'

'And you can take him into Alp de Montez?'

'Sure I can,' she said defensively. 'I'm a princess. Hoppy's out for adventure, and so am I.'

He stared at her for a moment while she finished the last of the champagne. And then stared regretfully into the empty glass. In a flash Griswold was out from behind his screen with a refill. The elderly man was now smiling, Nick saw. He hadn't smiled at him.

'I shouldn't,' Rose was saying.

'I'll be the wit-keeper,' he told her. 'Relax.'

'I'm not too sure I can trust you.'

'Aren't we almost cousins?'

'Cousins, if my mother hadn't played fast and loose. But, even if we were, family doesn't necessarily mean trust. Look at me and my sister.'

'Yeah, I don't understand that. Were you close when you were small?'

'When we were very young, yes. But my father thought Julianna was great, and he used to take her with him when he travelled. He travelled a lot, and I think it used to amuse him, to have such a gorgeous little girl calling him Papa. My mother and I stayed behind. Then we were booted out. I didn't mind,' she said diffidently. 'Much.' Then she shook herself. 'No. That sounds iffy. My mother and I had some really good times after we got out of the royal bit. We stayed with my Aunty Cath in London. The three of us always dreamed of going adventuring together, but Mum had rheumatoid arthritis and Aunty Cath owned six cats. That's a bit of a restriction where adventuring's concerned.'

'When did your mother die?'

'When I was twenty. Two years after Aunty Cath. A year after the last cat.'

'And then you met Max.'

'So I did,' she said diffidently. 'And he was great.'

'But an invalid?'

'Not when I first knew him. We had almost a year when he was in remission—we thought he was cured.'

'Did you marry him because you loved him?' Nick asked before he could help himself. 'Or because you felt sorry for him?'

Somewhat to his surprise, she answered seriously. 'You know, it was a whole lot of things,' she said. 'Max was twenty-six, and seemed older because he'd been ill. He was so pleased to be well again. It was just lovely—he wanted to try everything, do everything. And his family… We'd hardly even been a family, and after Mama and Aunty Cath there was no one. We went up to Yorkshire the first Christmas after we'd met, and it was such a welcome. The whole town, one big family. It was like coming home again. It was only afterwards that I felt…'

'Felt what?'

'Look, if Max had lived it would have been fine,' she said, sounding defensive again. 'But Max was larger than life. He had to be, he had too much living to do. The village had pooled together to get him the best medical treatment money could buy. As a community it was a huge commitment, and they loved him. When he died, well, there was only me, and they sort of transferred their loving to me.'

'And you're tired of loving?'

'A little bit,' she admitted, and sipped her champagne and smiled ruefully. 'I wouldn't mind a bit of adventuring. Me and Hoppy.'

He smiled back. Her smile was infectious even when it was rueful.

'And you,' she said curiously. 'What about your childhood? Erhard told me you're devoted to your foster mother.'

'Ruby's great.' But his words were curt. He didn't like people enquiring into his background.

The knowledge that Ruby's macramé class had been infiltrated gave him an odd feeling. Like he was exposed.

'Hey, if we're going to be married I need to know stuff about you,' she said. 'And you asked first.'

'So what do you need to know? How I like my toast buttered in the morning?'

'Butter your own toast, big boy,' she said, but she chuckled. 'No, but you know the sort of thing. I'd hate to find out that you have a fiancée and twelve kids.'

'No fiancée. No kids,' he said a bit too hastily. 'I'm sure Erhard would have told you if I had. But what about you? Did you and Max want kids?'

Her face closed, just like that.

'No.'

'I'm sorry. I didn't mean to pry.'

'That's three sorries in as many minutes from a lawyer,' she said, awed, and he thought she was changing the subject.

He went along with it though.

'I guess three sorries mean I'm at your mercy.'

'You know, I'm very sure you're not.' She smiled, but absently, and went back to hugging Hoppy. And looking out the window. Conversation over.

He left her to it, if reluctantly, retiring into a

pile of documents he needed to study. Even though he was taking a month off there were things he couldn't delegate. And time on planes was work time.

So he studied. Or he tried to study. Rose's nose stayed against the window. It was a very cute nose.

'What are you looking at?' he asked at last, but she didn't look around.

'Mountains.'

'Surely you've seen mountains before?'

'I used to see these peaks from the distance when I was a child.'

'You never went there?'

'Mama was an invalid. And my father…' She shrugged. 'He took Julianna.'

'But you've travelled?' he said, startled, and she shook her head.

'Only when we came to London. My mother was English, you see, so when my father sent her away she went to Aunty Cath. Then we were a bit stuck. But then, when I was twenty, Aunty Cath had a life-insurance policy—not very much, but enough. She'd stipulated I use it to travel. Mum seemed well, and the cats were all dead.'

Then she grinned. 'Hey, don't look sympathetic yet—we had some truly weird cats, and their collective age when they died was about a thousand. Anyway, Mum only had herself to look after and she was enthusiastic that I go. I had ten weeks' university holiday. Every holiday since I was fifteen I'd worked, trying to help. But this time it all seemed to fit. So I took a deep breath and flew to Australia, intending to backpack along the east coast. But the airline contacted me before I even reached Sydney. My mother had had a heart attack. Apparently she'd been having chest pain and hadn't told me. She'd seen specialists and still hadn't told me. She was dead before I got home. I used the last of Aunty Cath's nest egg to bury her and went back to university.'

He felt his own chest tighten. 'Didn't your father help?'

'You're kidding?' she said harshly. 'Of course not. He and Julianna stayed far away. Anyway…' She took a deep breath and moved on. 'How about you? How did you get to be an international lawyer?'

'Hard work.'

'If there was no money, you must have wanted it a lot.'

'I did.'

'Why?'

'I'm not sure,' he said, hesitating. She had him off balance. He'd not been questioned in such a personal way since… Well, since Ruby had sat him down after his secondary school results had come in, looked him straight in the eye and said,

'Tell me you don't want to be a lawyer because of the money?'

Was Rose asking the same question? Maybe she was.

'I don't really know,' he said, with the same reluctance he'd shown when Ruby had asked. But he'd been seventeen then. Now he was thirty six, and he'd had time to think his response through. 'I suspect it was a lot to do with my childhood. I felt helpless then—being taken from foster home to foster home. So I wanted security. Yes, I wanted a job where I could be in control. But there was also the issue of who my mother was. I knew about her royal background. It fascinated me. The only thing I had was a knowledge that the royal family of Alp de Montez was somehow my family. International law… Well, my job's helped to answer questions and make me feel as if the world is a smaller place.'

'Good answer,' she said, and she smiled.

'And vet science?'

'I always wanted a dog,' she said. 'And I was really fond of Aunty Cath's cats, even though they were collectively insane. Maybe that's a dumb reason for choosing a career, but there it is. I didn't have any wish to link internationally—even with Alp de Montez.'

'You've kept the language up?'

'I practiced with Italian and French language

tapes while I was at university—just for fun, because it seemed a shame to lose it. How about you?'

'My mother must have spoken the language when I was tiny. I hardly know how I got it, but it's there. I learned French and Italian at university as well. I gather the language of the Alp countries is a mishmash of both, so it seems we've both kept a little of our backgrounds.'

'Yeah, we're both royal,' she said absently. 'Um, there's snow on these mountains. And dots. Lots of colourful dots. Ski slopes?'

'These are the best ski-slopes in the world.'

'Do you ski?'

'Yes.'

'On these mountains?'

'Sometimes, yes.' International ski-fields were a good base for meeting the people he needed to know.

'Goodness,' she said faintly.

'Lots of people ski,' he said, knowing he sounded defensive, but not being able to stop himself.

'Not in my world they don't. They trudge round digging out livestock and swearing at the snow in general.'

'You've never skied?'

'I suspect there's a whole lot of stuff I've never done.' She turned to face him. 'Including marrying someone who skies in places like these.'

She shook her head and hugged her dog again. 'It's a whole new world.'

'Do you know what you're letting yourself in for?'

'No,' she said honestly. 'I know the people. I know there was lots that I loved. But I don't know the political set-up. Do you?'

'I've researched this well, yes.'

'It's more than I have,' she conceded.

'You just jumped.'

'That's right. Ran, more like.'

'It does sound appealing,' he said. 'Playing princess.'

'I don't expect I shall play princess,' she said absently. 'As you said, it's dumb to eat caviar. I guess if I have authority then I'll start by doing things like selling this ostentatious aeroplane.'

But it seemed she'd said the wrong thing. The screen in front of them was put aside with a decisive click. The man who'd been serving them, Griswold, was staring at them in consternation.

'You must not,' he said in his own language. And he sounded desperate.

Rose frowned, confused by his sudden interjection, slipping effortlessly into the language that matched his. 'We mustn't sell this aeroplane?'

'No. I... Not yet.'

'I guess it's your job,' she said, confused.

'It's not my job,' the elderly man told her. 'Or

not very often. I'm sorry. This is none of my business. I shouldn't have said. Your dinner is almost ready.'

'So tell us why we shouldn't sell the plane,' Nick asked, moving easily into the language as well.

'We need you to be the royal couple,' Griswold said simply. 'Nothing else will save the country.' And he flicked back the screen and went back to work.

No more was said until the meal was served— magnificent beef steak, which spoke heaps of Griswold's skill in cooking in confined spaces. No pre-packed airline food this.

There was chocolate mousse to follow, and espresso coffee. Finally as he cleared the coffee cups away Griswold's severe face relaxed a little. But as he reached for Rose's cup she took his wrist and held.

'Tell me what you mean about wanting us to be a royal couple,' she said.

'*Madame*, I can't.'

'You can't do what?'

'I…' He shook his head. 'There's orders.'

'From who?'

'From Monsieur Jacques. The husband of your sister.'

'Orders to do what?'

'To tell you nothing,' he said miserably. 'To let you do this mock-marriage thing.'

'It's not a mock marriage,' Rose said, frowning more. 'It's a real one.'

'It's not,' Griswold said simply. 'I've been over-hearing. What Julianna and Jacques have been telling the people is right. That this is a marriage of convenience.'

'It's still a marriage.'

'Yes, but there's more,' he said unhappily. 'Reports are that this marriage is a sham, and so is any goodwill you might have towards our people. You're outsiders. You'll sign the right papers and then disappear again. No wrongs will be righted. Taxes will continue to be bled from the people and sent overseas. Our country will be worse off.'

'That's not why we're here,' Nick said, frowning as much as Rose was. 'Erhard Fritz—'

'Erhard Fritz is being discredited by the government-controlled press,' Griswold said. 'There's been a smear campaign. The press is portraying you both as upstart outsiders. You, *monsieur*, with vaguely sinister intentions and you, *madame*, as a greedy widow.'

'Why are you telling us this?' Rose said slowly, her eyes not leaving Griswold's face.

'Maybe…because of the dog?' he said unhappily. 'I know that sounds nonsense, but my daughter has a dog such as this one. I listened to you telling *monsieur* how you took in the dog, and I thought this can't be a woman such as the press describes. I remembered the stories of you as a child. The press was fairer then, not controlled by the Council. You were always described as a tomboy, more interested in animals than in learning society manners. Then the way you both gave thanks. Little things, but…I heard you talking about a marriage of convenience, and I thought "it doesn't fit".'

'It's a way of repairing the damage,' Nick said. 'We can set in place reforms.'

'Not if the people rise up against you,' Griswold said. 'Which they will if they think you're here for your own gain. If you sell this plane straight away, they'll think it's a first act to siphon money. Things have been said, dreadful things.'

'I've heard nothing of this,' Nick snapped.

'Jacques and his friends are too clever to use the main newsprints to spread the worst of the rumours,' the man said unhappily. 'But rumours have been sweeping the country nevertheless. And people like Erhard, people of sense, have been effectively silenced.'

'There's not a lot we can do about it,' Rose said doubtfully. 'We were told it would be simple.'

'You need to get the people on side,' Griswold said. 'People like me. Working people. All of us. I do have some English. All the time I've been cooking, I've been listening to you. You both can speak our language. That's wonderful. *Madame*, the people were fond of you once, as a child. They'll remember that. You have the little dog. As you walk out of this plane, you need to look happy to be in the country. Happy to be home. You need to speak to as many people as possible. Ordinary people. You need to see and be seen. And you need to hold hands all the time. Speak to each other as a married couple. Don't appear to have heard a single thing that I've just told you. And…'

'And?'

'And let the people know that you mean well. And that you're not trying to deceive them. Let them know that you're about to enter into a marriage.'

CHAPTER FIVE

THEY landed soon after, questions unresolved. 'I think that my wife's cousin will be driving the royal car,' Griswold told them as the plane came to a standstill. 'He will wish you well. As I do.' But his contact with them was over. He stayed aboard, unhappily disappearing into the background as they emerged onto Alp de Montez soil.

They weren't sure what to expect when they arrived. After Erhard's silence, Nick had been contacted by someone calling himself the palace Chief of Staff, telling them he was taking care of the arrangements for their arrival. 'There'll be some form of official reception,' he'd told them, and when they stepped off the jet that was exactly what happened.

There were a couple of dozen military officers standing to stiff attention, and a middle-aged man in hugely decorated dress-regalia stepped forward to greet them.

'Good afternoon,' the man said in stiff English.

'Welcome to Alp de Montez, Your Royal Highnesses. Do you wish to inspect the guard now?'

'No,' Nick said before Rose could open her mouth. Then he looked at Rose. 'We don't want to inspect the guard, do we, sweetheart?'

Sweetheart?

Rose blinked. And then she got the message. What Griswold had said on the plane was that these people were expecting a marriage of convenience, a marriage designed to fleece the country. Somehow they had to change that image.

She swallowed, then grabbed Nick's hand and held tightly. 'We might,' she said. Then, 'I can't tell you how pleased we are to be here,' she said, in a voice that carried across the tarmac to the assembled troops, speaking in the Italian-French mix that was the country's own dialect. 'I loved this country as a child,' she said. 'I needed to leave with my mother when I was fifteen—you know my parents were separated?—and Nick was orphaned early. That's left us ignorant of what we should know of our heritage. So you'll need to excuse us as we find our feet. You'll have to teach us, but we're here to learn.'

Then she smiled sweetly at the greeting official, who was looking stunned, and just a little bit horrified. 'Thank you so much for meeting us,' she said, and before he knew what she was about she'd handed Hoppy over to him, then kissed the astounded man on both cheeks. 'I was sure we'd be welcome,' she said. 'You're truly kind.'

Then, before the official could say a word, while Nick stood on the tarmac with the warm evening breeze adding to his sense of unreality— even though it was late spring it had been freezing back at Heathrow—Rose grabbed his hand and towed him over to the assembled troops. She smiled at the first soldier and asked his name. Before Nick knew it, they were working their way down the line, greeting every soldier individually, taking their hands and shaking them. Forcing them to lower their guns as they did. And Rose was giving each of them her very nicest smile.

By the time they'd finished Nick was feeling gobsmacked. Maybe they all were. The line didn't look nearly as formal, and the stiff, unsmiling faces were, well, trying not to smile, but smiling for all that.

'So who do we meet next?' she asked, still beaming, returning to the official and Hoppy. She took Hoppy back from the stunned officer, thanking him with a smile.

'Your limousine's waiting to take you to the palace,' the man said stiffly.

'I don't know your name,' Rose said.

'I'm Chief of Staff,' the man said.

'But a name?' Rose said gently, smiling some

more, and the man stared at her like she was speaking gobbledegook. 'I'm Rose,' she said, giving him an easy example. 'This is Nick.'

'Sir. Madam.'

'Yes, but we have names too,' she said, fixing him with a smile that took Nick aback even further. This wasn't some wilting violet. This was a woman determined to make her point. A woman starting her adventuring.

'Jean Dupeaux,' the man muttered, and she smiled some more.

'It's lovely to meet you, Jean. If you're our Chief of Staff, then I guess we'll see lots of you. This is my dog, Hoppy. Are you coming with us in the limousine?'

'I… No.'

'That's a shame,' she said brightly. 'I guess we'll see you at the palace, then. Does the driver know where to go?'

'Of course.' He seemed offended.

'I'm so sorry. Of course he does. You'll have to forgive us a lot as we learn our way round,' she told him. 'I have so much to remember. But don't worry. We're here for the long haul, and we'll get it right in the end.'

They didn't speak for the first couple of minutes in the limousine. It was as if both needed to catch their breath. Certainly Nick did. What had just happened seemed extraordinary. A salute

of arms to start with, and then Rose's perfor-
mance.

'Griswold was right,' she said at last, staring out
the window at the passing scenery. They were
less than a mile from the airport, travelling
towards the nearby city, but the towering, snow-
capped mountains were breathtaking. In the fields
beside the road the farmers were gathering in the
hay, forming bales in the way farmers had done
for a thousand years.

'It seems we've been made enemies before we
even arrived,' she said slowly. 'How did that
happen?'

'Maybe we should have expected it,' he said.

What else should they have expected? The
looks they'd been given by the troops before
Rose's impromptu greeting session had been
aloof and disdainful. This was a tiny segment of
the army, and the army must be powerful. Where
did the army come into this?

Rose was looking as thoughtful as he was. And
there was a trace of fear behind her eyes.

Hoppy was on her knee. He wriggled off,
crossed the gap in the seat between them and put
a paw tentatively on Nick's knee.

'He thinks you need a hug,' Rose said.

'I don't need a hug,' he said, stunned.

'I might,' she said diffidently.

'I'm not sure that's wise.'

'Right,' she said, and lifted Hoppy back into her arms and hugged him. 'Sorry.'

Why couldn't he have hugged her? Why did she have him so off-balance? They were in trouble together. It made sense to be able to give each other comfort.

But if he hugged her now…

Don't go there.

'We need to do some fast footwork,' he said, trying desperately to move forward. Past the emotional. 'Rose, we know nothing. Where the hell is Erhard?'

'I was sure he'd meet us,' she said.

His legal mind was trying to sort things. Things other than how close Rose was sitting to him. Important stuff.

Only he was having a huge amount of trouble persuading his mind to think past her. She was messing with his equilibrium in a way he didn't understand.

Think. Think!

Back in London this succession had seemed reasonable—even sensible. Now it seemed fraught. Two people in a strange land, threatening those in power.

'Maybe we need to bail out for a bit and rethink,' he said dubiously. 'Damn, I didn't foresee this. I had my people—'

'My people?'

'My colleagues. I'm not an international lawyer for nothing. They checked this place. There's never been armed insurrection in any of the Alp countries. There didn't seem a threat. But now…'

'I'm not going home,' Rose said.

'We might have to.'

'I'm not going home,' she said again, and hugged Hoppy tighter. Hoppy gave a doleful canine sigh—he was obviously accustomed to being an emotional squeeze-bag. 'I might be persuaded to treat Hawaiian animals, or something similar, but no more in Yorkshire.'

'What's wrong with Yorkshire?'

'Too much family,' she muttered. 'Alright if you want a career as a battery hen. And, by the way, that includes you,' she said, glaring as he gazed at her in astonishment. 'I don't think I said, but you try and protect me and I refuse to be responsible for my actions. No matter that we're getting married—name only. No family. No ties. And I want to get this place sorted. Right. What's next?' And she looked so fierce that he held up his hands in mock surrender.

What a statement! His desire to hug her should have stopped right there. Only for some dumb reason it intensified. He had to fight to make himself agree.

'Sure,' he managed. 'That's how I feel too.' Or was it?

'Just so you know,' she said, still glowering. 'But, even if I didn't feel like that, I still wouldn't run. Yes, I got concerned when I didn't hear from Erhard this week, and I was spooked when the press arrived, but I've cut my ties now and I'm over it. So move on. We'll get some plans in place and do what Erhard wanted. Now.'

She looked so fierce that he smiled. But he was thinking hard. What lay ahead seemed much more of a challenge than it had seemed back home, but maybe he, like Rose, was glad to move on. For different reasons. She was leaving family. He was leaving a vacuum.

No. Just boredom. He wanted a challenge.

And it didn't hurt that he'd face this challenge with Rose beside him. He just had to resist the desire to…hug.

No. What he really wanted to do was kiss her until her toes curled. Or his toes curled.

What he really needed, on the other hand, was a cold shower. If he did anything so dumb she'd slug him into the middle of next week.

'We need to get meetings in place straight away,' he said slowly, managing to think a bit further. 'We'll get the armed-forces chiefs to the palace. Let them know what we intend. Figure out where they stand. We need to speak to each individual councillor.'

'So you will stay?' she said, and he glanced at her in surprise.

'For as long as it takes, Rose, yes. I promised, and I'll keep my word.'

'It's only…I'm aware that it's me who's supposed to be sovereign,' she muttered. 'But I don't have the skills.'

'I suspect neither of us have the skills. But no one else does either, so it's fight through it or run. You've said you won't run, and neither will I.'

'Thank you.'

He smiled. 'You know, from all accounts, prince consorts never had such a bad time of it in the past,' he said. 'All that wheeling and dealing behind closed doors. I'll be the one who'll tell you whose head to chop off, you do the dirty work, and then you get the flack and not me.'

'Oh, great.'

'I'm truly noble,' he said, and he managed to grin.

She tried not to smile. She failed.

She looked enchanting, he thought. The more he looked at her the more enchanted he became. She was still huddled in her oversized duffel coat—not because she needed its warmth, he suspected, but because she found the familiar smell of it comforting. Hoppy certainly did. The little dog was huddling against her, under her coat, only his nose exposed in quivering anxiety.

Me and my dog against the world.

'I don't think this'll work if you're prince consort,' she said softly.

He thought about it for a moment. 'That's what the whole idea is.'

'No, it's not. I don't think we should be crown and deputy.'

'I'm sorry, but—'

'Hey, you know I'm really not royal,' she said, interrupting him. 'My mother was married and then left to fend for herself. My father married her on a whim, tired of her within a year and then, as far as I can tell, never touched her again. He went from scandal to scandal, while my mother stayed in the castle and cared for the old Prince. There were visitors, and I was born with red hair, and I'll not be judging her for it. She must have been unbearably lonely.' She touched her flaming head and grinned. 'So there you are. I was born royal but I'm not really royal, whereas you… Your mother really was a princess.'

'Yes, but…' He was getting distracted. By her hair.

'But what?'

'It's the way it has to work,' he said with difficulty. 'It's you who's in line for the throne.'

'But you want it,' she said thoughtfully. 'You're aching to get in there and do stuff. You can't do that if you're not a full partner.'

'I don't think you can devolve authority until you have it,' he said, striving to keep it light.

'I guess not,' she whispered, and then her voice firmed a little. 'I guess I have to take it on. I can cope. I have before.' He watched her face became more resolute.

David aiming his slingshot?

They were reaching the outskirts of the city now. It was Saturday at twilight, the light just starting to fade.

'Where does everyone here go on a Saturday night?' she asked suddenly, and then as Nick looked blank she reached forward and slid back the glass partitioning them from the driver.

'If you and your family were wanting a fun night out tonight,' she said to the driver, 'Where would you go?'

'Madame?' the driver said, confused, and she repeated her question.

'What's a good local drinking place in the heart of the city?' she said. 'Maybe with a band playing. Is there somewhere like that?'

'The army officers use Maison d'Etre.'

'No, not the army,' she said, while Nick stayed as confused as the driver. 'You. Or the farmers we just saw. Where do most people go?'

'I live just two miles from here,' the man said dubiously. 'It's Saturday night. It's harvest time and the weather's good. The time-honoured local tradition at this time of year is to gather down at the river bank not far from here, or at other picnic spots round the country.' He hesitated. 'There's not the money for families to go to pubs any more. Taxes are terrible. The army and the politicians use the restaurants and pubs, but most of them, well, they've closed for lack of patronage.'

'And down at the river?'

'That's where we go,' he said simply. 'Each district has its own meeting place. We go there or we stay home.'

'But the young ones, they go to the pictures and things?'

'If you're in a well-paid job. But there are few well-paid jobs.'

'So if we wanted to meet the people…'

'Maybe you could go on the television,' he said doubtfully.

'We don't want to do that,' Rose said. 'Not yet.' She visibly swallowed a gulp. 'I don't think I'd be very good at television.'

'So what are you thinking?' Nick said uneasily, watching the set of her face. This was a woman who, having decided to do something, went for it. Even facing television.

'I'm not going back to Yorkshire,' she said. 'Not for a lack of gumption on my part.'

'No one's making you.'

'Yes, but the main reason I can come here is

that I have an imperative,' she said. 'I have an imperative here, but I also have an imperative back in Yorkshire. I haven't told you what that imperative is, but believe me facing a firing squad at dawn looks pretty good in comparison. No. We get proactive. Did you have to wear a suit?'

'Did you have to wear a duffel coat?'

'A duffel coat's more appropriate than what you're wearing,' she retorted. 'Lose the tie. Do you have a jacket in your baggage?'

'I'm not sure where our baggage is.'

'It's being brought separately,' the driver said, bemused, watching them through the rear-view mirror.

'If we wanted to go to your picnic…' Rose said slowly, looking ahead and behind at their convoy. There were twelve uniformed army-officers in front of them on motor bikes. There were twelve behind. 'Do you suppose they'd arrest us if we stopped down at the river?'

'Madame, we can't stop.'

'Yes, we can,' she said.

'My orders are to take you straight to the palace.'

'And whose orders are those?' she asked, and all of a sudden she was haughty. The driver stared at her in astonishment—and so did Nick. Then the eyes of the two men met. A small moment of male empathy. Two male shrugs, and the driver gave a small smile.

'You want to go to our picnic?'

'We need to meet the people,' she said. 'This is the fastest way to do that, right?'

'I guess.'

'Then our escort can come too. But we don't have food for a picnic. I won't be a freeloader.'

'The people will share.'

'I'm not going to my first picnic in Alp de Montez as a freeloader,' Rose said. 'My fiancé agrees with me.'

'Do I?' said Nick.

'Of course you do—darling,' she said. 'Now, what can we do?'

'If I might make a suggestion…' The limousine driver was looking at her as if she had two heads. So was Nick.

'Suggest away,' she said.

'If you were to produce, say, a keg or two of beer… Beer's expensive and rationed.'

'Beer's rationed?' she said incredulously.

'Do you have maybe a Diner's Card?'

'I bet my fiancé does.'

'Do you, sir?'

'Eh?' Nick said, getting more startled by the minute. This was a seriously startling woman.

She grinned. 'My fiancé will pay you,' she said. 'Erhard told me you're seriously rich. I'm not, but I'm working on it. Soon I'll be a princess, but I'm waiting on my first wages. I need a loan of a keg until pay-day.'

It was too much. They were sitting in the back of a royal limousine, escorted by armed troops, heading to a palace with who knew what reception, and she was calmly negotiating a loan of a keg or two of beer.

He chuckled. The driver chuckled. Nick delved obediently into his wallet and produced his Diner's Card.

'So how will this help?' Rose asked the driver.

'The husband of my wife's cousin works as a delivery driver to one of the army hotels,' the driver said, moving into the spirit of the thing with enthusiasm. 'If I radio your card details he can organise a keg to be here within the hour.'

'Two kegs,' Nick said, deciding he could be expansive too. 'And lemonade for the kids.'

'A keg of lemonade?'

'I don't have a clue how it comes,' Nick admitted. 'We'll leave that to your wife's cousin's husband. Tell him to bring what he thinks a gathering will need. I guess you know the numbers. Though how we know we can trust you...'

'There are very few people in the higher echelons you can trust,' the driver said flatly. Then he smiled again. 'But we're not accustomed to seeing our royalty in overcoats that smell a little like the farmyard. And while you were inspecting the troops Griswold told me we might hope. Things are desperate here. We're willing to take a chance on you.'

'You won't get sacked if you deviate?' Rose asked.

'By the time our escort has time to respond, we'll be there. I'll be following your direct orders. Maybe you organised this with Erhard long since, no? Not with me.'

'Not with you,' Rose said firmly.

The driver looked at her again for a long minute in the rear-view mirror and then he gave a decisive nod. He picked up his radio and spoke fast, quoting Nick's Diner's Club card number, ordering his supplies. Then he handed back Nick's card.

'Thank you both.' He smiled at Nick via the rear-view mirror. 'There's a jacket under the front seat you can borrow,' he told him. 'It's not as disreputable as your fiancée's, but it will have to do. Hold on please.'

With a squeal of brakes the car turned at ninety degrees and proceeded calmly down to the river bank, with Nick wondering what he'd got himself into. And it wasn't just the situation that was startling him. It was this woman beside him. And how he was starting to react to her.

Rose. Potential princess. Potential wife.

Up until now he'd hardly thought about the wife bit. It hadn't seemed relevant.

Now, though, when he should be thinking a thousand other things, that was the word that was drifting around his head, like a chink of light through clouds, a tiny glimmer of possibility.

Wife.

CHAPTER SIX

THERE had to be argument from their minders. Of course there did. There was a moment's peace, before their escort of motor bikes reassembled, veered off the highway and roared after them. Then the head of the squad—Jean Dupeaux— came alongside their limousine and gestured angrily for the driver to pull over. Nick's errant thoughts were dragged back to the here and now with a vicious jolt as the bike nosed sharply in front of the car, causing their driver to brake and veer onto the verge.

But not stop. The driver was starting to look as determined as, well, as determined as Rose.

The bike jerked back so it was driving alongside. Rose let down her window, put out her head and yelled, 'Our driver's following our instructions, Monsieur Dupeaux. We just want to see the river.'

'You must pull over,' Dupeaux shouted, and Rose smiled happily, waved and closed the window.

What was the Chief of Staff doing, riding motor bikes? Nick thought. And then, more nervously, *what is going on here*?

Dupeaux veered in front of the car again. The driver skilfully pulled out and overtook him.

What the outcome would have been if they'd had to go further Nick couldn't tell, but they were already turning to where the cliffs along the river-bank formed what seemed almost a natural amphitheatre. Willows hung over the slow moving river. There were ruins of some ancient castle high on the cliffs. A few cars were parked under the trees, but mostly there were horses and carts. And people.

There was real poverty in this country, Nick thought. Horses and carts might look picturesque, but these weren't men and women using their horses and carts for pleasure. These horses were workhorses, and every single man and woman—and even the adolescents—looked as if they'd spent a long, hard day in the fields. No luxury of going home to a long, hot bath and a change of clothes, but still they'd assembled to enjoy the evening.

The people turned as one at the arrival of the limousine, with its trailing queue of motor bikes. Their jaws dropped in astonishment.

And then displeasure. Nick saw the moment their surprise turned to resentment as they recognised the coat of arms on the limousine, as they realised what the outriders represented.

They shouldn't be here, he thought, his astute mind working things through fast. If there was antagonism to royalty, how would they react to the surprise visit of two rank outsiders?

But, before he could stop her, Rose was out of the car. He climbed out afterwards, but was called back. 'Sir!' The driver sounded insistent. He was handing him a shabby leather-jacket.

'I'll get it back from you some time,' he said diffidently. 'Just don't lose it.' And then he smiled. 'By the way, the lady said lose the tie.'

Lose the tie. Right. He hauled his tie off, undid a couple of buttons, shrugged on the jacket and rounded the car to join Rose.

'Hi,' she was saying as the people stared at her. The uniformed motor-bike riders were coming in now, gathering in a cluster around the car. But they didn't kill their engines. The noise was overpowering. And there were horses…

Nick saw the danger. 'Kill the engines. Now!' he ordered, but the damage had been done.

One of the horses—the one nearest the bikes—was shifting sideways in its traces, clearly panicked. It reared once and then grounded, backing. Its eyes were rolling, nostrils flaring.

There was a child in the cart behind it. *No!*

But Rose had seen. Closer than Nick, she could get there faster. She dumped Hoppy unceremoniously on the ground and strode swiftly forward to grab the horses bridle. She steadied it, then tugged it sideways, hauling its head around so it was forced to yield the force in its hindquarters.

Even Nick, who scarcely knew one end of a horse from another, could see this was an expert. In one swift movement she'd defused a potentially deadly situation.

'Hush,' she told the horse into the sudden stillness, speaking in the local dialect. 'Quiet, now. Hush.' Then, as the horse settled, she spoke to the people around them. 'I'm sorry. I should have known there'd be horses here. I forgot the bikes would follow.'

As the child's mother darted forward to retrieve her daughter from the cart, Rose took her time, soothing the big horse, scratching behind his ears, whispering reassurance, waiting until the flare of panic faded from his eyes. Nick could only watch, entranced. Every moment he spent with this woman meant he saw another facet of her. She was amazing. She took all the time she needed to settle the big animal, then handed the bridle over to his owner.

Hoppy pawed at her leg in some indignation. She picked him up and stroked him behind his ears as well.

She had the absolute attention of every person there.

'I'm so sorry,' she told the people around them.

'Nick and I have just come from the airport. I'm not sure if you know, but I'm Rose-Anitra. I left here when I was fifteen, but I was never able to leave the palace grounds very much before then, so I don't know you. This is my fiancé, Nikolai de Montez. Son of the old Prince's daughter, Zia. We've been told that we stand to inherit the throne. We're here to talk it through, and we want to meet some of the locals. Don't we, Nick?' She turned and smiled at him, and he walked forward until he was by her side. It was what she seemed to want.

Which suited him. This was a woman to be proud of.

A wife to be proud of?

Equal partners? The thought was suddenly seductive for all sorts of reasons.

'I'm a veterinary surgeon,' she told the assemblage, tucking her hand confidingly in Nick's—a gesture of intimacy which jolted him still further. 'So we should know better than to scare your animals. This was just a whim, to stop here.'

'You have no business being here,' Dupeaux shouted. 'These people don't want you.'

That might have been a foolish thing to say, Nick decided, watching the faces of the crowd around them. Rose looked a chit of a thing in her too-big jacket and holding her lame dog. She'd just quieted a massive horse. She had the advantage of looking a bit of a stray herself.

Dupeaux was big and uniformed and brusque. Authority personified. 'Get back in the car, woman,' he snapped, and there was a visible ripple of dissent. 'Leave these people be. They don't want you here.'

With one harsh order, this man had made Rose an underdog, and from all he'd seen so far Rose wasn't anyone's underdog.

'Erhard Fritz told us that we were wanted here,' Rose said gently but firmly, stating something that was out of her control. 'Erhard said this country needed us.'

'We don't need royalty,' someone shouted from the back of the crowd, and Rose faltered.

Time to lend a hand, Nick thought. He couldn't stay being a complete wimp.

'Rose and I never thought there was any need for us to be in this country,' Nick said, loudly, urgently, speaking as Rose had spoken in the native tongue. 'You know, we never thought we'd inherit the throne. We don't understand what your problems are. But Erhard came to find us. He's shown us what's being done in your neighbouring countries—Alp d'Azur and Alp d'Estella. He says a sympathetic royalty could make that happen here. We could organise things so the country could self-rule as a democracy. Erhard's convinced us to try. Of course, if we're wrong, if we're truly not wanted, then we'll go.'

Silence. Not a man, woman or child moved.

Behind them, the troops shifted uneasily. These riders were the same men who'd greeted them at the airport. Rose had charmed them.

Here she'd done it again. Maybe.

Rose's grip on his fingers tightened. It felt good, he thought. It felt…right.

'What's your dog's name?' a little boy called out from the front of the crowd, and Rose smiled.

'He's Hoppy. Because of his leg. He can hop better than any dog I know.'

'He doesn't look like a royal dog.'

'I tried to get him to wear a tiara,' Rose said, and grinned. 'But Hoppy thought he looked like a sissy.'

Amazingly there was a ripple of laughter.

'Can he play with my dog?' the little boy asked. He motioned to a half-grown collie, thin and straggly but wagging its disreputable tail with the air of a dog expecting a good time.

'Of course,' Rose said, and put Hoppy down.

The two dogs eyed each other warily, and then proceeded to sniff the most important part of their anatomy.

The shock and sullen resentment of the crowd was turning to smiles.

'Are you really a prince and princess?' someone called.

'We're the son and daughter of the old Prince's children,' Nick replied. 'We haven't been in direct line to the throne, so until we come into succession we've no title. Rose-Anitra is first in line to the throne before her sister, Julianna, and I come after her. If our claim to the throne succeeds, then Rose would be Crown Princess and I'd be…' He hesitated. 'You know, I'm not sure what I'd be.'

'Mr Crown Prince?' someone called, and there was more laughter.

'Crown Consort,' someone else called. 'You'd be Crown Consort, and Earl de Montez as well. I think you already are. There's no one else to inherit the title.'

'What about Julianna's husband?' someone else called.

'He's not royal,' someone else snapped. 'No matter what airs he might give himself.'

'Will you get back in the car?' Dupeaux snapped, and he sounded furious. He took a step towards Rose which might or might not have been menacing, but suddenly Nick was standing in front of Rose. He wasn't alone with his protective instincts. In a flash there were half a dozen burly men between Nick and the officer.

'It's you and your bullies who aren't wanted here, Dupeaux,' someone called to the officer in charge, and the man's face darkened in fury.

'Look, this is a private party,' Nick said, speaking quickly, knowing he had to deflect confrontation. 'Rose and I don't have a right to be here unasked. We've ordered a couple of kegs of beer and a few other things, to make the evening a bit more fun for you. They'll be here any minute, whether or not we stay. No matter. We just wanted to say hello. Now maybe we should leave.'

'But we'd like you to stay. And you can share our picnic,' someone called.

'And ours.'

'And mine.'

'These men are our escort,' Rose said, taking courage again, holding Nick's hand tighter and smiling towards the men on bikes. 'Can they stay too?'

'No,' Dupeaux snapped. 'They're on duty.'

'Then isn't it lucky we're not?' Rose said, and tugged Nick forward to where an elderly lady had unpacked her basket on a rug on the grass. 'Are they chocolate éclairs? My favourite.' She turned back to the officer and smiled her sweetest smile. 'If you leave us the limousine, we'll make our own way home. Thank you for escorting us so far.'

Dupeaux had no choice. There were a couple of hundred people gathered here, and more arriving every minute. To use force would escalate the situation in a way he might not be able to control. So he and his men disappeared in a roar of diesel engine that had the horses rearing again. Almost as soon as they'd gone, a battered truck turned into the clearing.

'Two kegs of beer, crates of lemonade, and wine for the ladies,' the man driving the truck said. 'Pierre said you were ordering for a party so I took the liberty…'

'Brilliant,' Rose said, beaming. Only the way she was still holding tight to Nick's hand let Nick know that underneath this outward show of bravado she was more nervous than he was. But she wasn't letting on. 'We have a party.'

And a party they had.

It would have been a good party anyway, Nick thought as the evening wore on. Anyone who could play any sort of instrument had been dragged into the toe-tappingly good band. The food seemed generous and plentiful—great home-cooking. The beer and lemonade and wine flowed plentifully. And Rose worked the crowd.

Actually, they both did. Nick had been in enough international situations to know how to make small-talk, to ask the right questions, to keep things flowing smoothly without treading on sensitivities. He'd been trained to do it. Rose did it naturally.

It almost felt as if he was back at work, Nick

thought as he moved among the crowd, but there was a huge difference here. For whoever he spoke to in this gathering was trying desperately to find out about him, to gauge his interest as being genuine or not, and to discover whether Rose felt the same. He and Rose had spent so little time together that he could only hope they were now presenting a united front. They were forced apart—there were too many people wanting to talk to them to allow them to stay as a couple—but he was aware that people were talking easily to her, laughing with her, enjoying her presence.

As he was. She had style, he thought, the sort of style that couldn't be taught. They'd had people come into the firm who'd lacked people skills, and no amount of training had given it to them. It required genuine interest in the person they were talking to. It could never be feigned.

'She's a lovely young woman,' an elderly man said to him, and he realised that he'd turned to glance at Rose and maybe watched for longer than he'd intended. Well, why not? The farmer was watching her too, and his face showed he was as appreciative as Nick was.

'She's a damned sight more attractive than her sister,' the old man said, and that brought Nick up with a start. There were factors here that he hadn't yet met—threats? Their escort had disappeared. The powers that be would be uncomfortable with what was happening right now, he thought. What would they do?

'Please…' It was a young man, just arrived on a shabby motor-scooter. He had a camera slung around his neck. Beside him was an intense-looking young woman with pad and pencil.

'We had a call,' the young man said. 'To say you were here.'

'Lew and his friends run a newspaper,' the old man said.

'It's supposed to be illegal,' someone else said. 'Only the government can't shut it down because they don't charge. It comes out as two or four pages every month.'

'With things the government don't want us to know,' someone else added.

So he and Rose were interviewed, a professional, insightful interview that Nick realised was sympathetic to the people's cause. The journalist wasn't interested so much in Nick and Rose as what they intended to do. She was interested in them as a means to lessen the plight of the men and women around them.

As was everyone else. As the interview progressed, the crowd around them fell silent. Someone signalled the musicians to put aside their instruments. Every ear was tuned to what they were saying. As Nick outlined the changes in Alp d'Azur and Alp d'Estella—their neighbouring principalities—and their hopes that the same changes could be made here, there was a ripple of approval through the crowd.

Finally the reporter tucked her notebook in her jacket, smiling her approval. Interview over. Now for the photographs.

'Dance,' someone called. 'That'll make a great photograph.'

The musicians obediently struck up again, but not in the lively folk music they'd been playing. They played a slow waltz so the photographer would have time to focus.

Once more Rose was in his arms.

'We're doing okay,' he murmured into her hair as he led her round the grassy makeshift dance-floor. No one else was dancing—all eyes were on them.

'I know,' she said, but she sounded uncomfortable.

'So what's the problem?'

'I'm thinking… It feels weird.'

'The whole situation?'

'Dancing with you.'

He paused, lost his timing, made a recovery. The youth with the camera was moving around them, taking shots from all angles.

'It feels okay to me,' he said cautiously. 'You're not a bad dancer.'

'Thank you,' she said, but she didn't smile.

'So what's weird?'

'Nothing.'

'You just said…'

'I know what I said,' she snapped, and concentrated on the dance for a little. But she didn't need to concentrate.

'Um…Rose?'

'Yes?' She sounded seriously annoyed.

'I'm not sure what I've done wrong here.'

'You haven't done anything,' she said crossly. 'That's the trouble.'

'Right.'

'It doesn't make any sense to me either.'

'No.'

There was a moment's silence. Another circuit of the dance ground.

'You're very good,' she said at last, stiffly, and he thought about that for a bit, aware that it behoved him to tread cautiously.

'At dancing?' he asked at last.

'At this,' she said. 'At the political bit.'

'I was thinking the same thing about you.'

'No, but you're smooth,' she said. 'You do it like a professional. I don't know how much it means.'

'I don't understand.'

'It's occurred to me that I'm not really sure who you are,' she said. 'You're like a piece of veneered furniture, polished on the outside, but what's underneath?'

'Wormwood,' he said promptly, and felt her smile.

'I don't think so. But you're so…smooth.'

'And that worries you?'

'You see, I find you incredibly attractive,' she said.

As dance conversation that was a real show-stopper. His feet faltered.

'Do mind your steps,' she said kindly. 'The photographer's documenting your every move.'

'I've never been told before…'

'That you're incredibly attractive? I find that hard to believe.'

He was back in step now, and found himself smiling, responding to her laughter. 'It's a guy's line.'

'A pick-up line,' she agreed. 'That's why I thought I ought to say it.'

'You're trying to pick me up?'

'The opposite.' They turned right by the youth with the camera, and she beamed into the lens. 'It just occurred to me, then, watching you.'

'Watching me dance?'

'No, watching you talk to everyone. Watching you make people smile. Watching you make people believe that you're sincere and that you have their best interests at heart.'

'That's a problem?' he said cautiously, and she nodded.

'Yes.'

'You want to tell me why?'

'Because I'm starting to believe you. And it doesn't help that you dance so well.'

'You want me to dance badly?'

'I don't know what I want. All I know is that we're being forced to spend time together as a couple and it's starting to scare me. And because you'll be used to dating and I'm not…'

'I'm losing the thread here,' he said, and she looked exasperated. How they could be holding a personal conversation in the midst of such an audience was beyond him, but Rose was speaking to him as if they were completely alone. As if whatever she was talking about had to be said urgently. It had to be said now.

'I met Max in second year of vet school. I was just turned twenty and my mother had just died. Max was my second-ever boyfriend. My first was a guy called Robert who I fell for because he had a really cool sportscar. But that's it, my dating history, so brief you could write it on a postage stamp.'

'I'm still not following,' he said cautiously.

'You don't have to follow,' she said, and sighed. 'That's it. I just want to make it clear that I'm not the least bit interested in a relationship, so even if I do laugh at anything you say, and even if I do find you attractive, then it's up to you to call a halt. Use a bucket of cold water if necessary, but please, let's not let this relationship go any further than it already has.'

'No,' he said blankly. 'Right.'

'Yeah, and I can tell you think I'm forward,' she said. 'Or scatty, which is just as bad. But I do need to say that I'm not the least bit interested in a relationship. I'm not saying never—that'd be extreme, and I might want to stick my toe in the water in later life. But not for at least five years. I want freedom. Absolute freedom.'

'Just so I know,' he said.

'Yes.'

'For my information.'

'Yes.'

'So no hitting on anyone, then?'

'You can hit on anyone you like. Just not me.'

'But we are getting married, right?'

'Yes, but that's got nothing to do with the rest of it. I'm sorry,' she said, suddenly contrite. 'I'm sure you don't have the slightest intention of showing interest in me, so I sound really dumb and really gauche, and totally out of order. So I'll shut up.'

'Um…right.'

So what was that all about—the chemistry between them, the way she felt in his arms?

Was she feeling this too—almost overwhelmed?

Maybe it was a good thing to bring it out in the

open, he thought cautiously. He didn't want relationships either.

Did he?

They danced on, but they were now no longer alone. The cameraman had finished, and the makeshift dance-floor was filling as other couples joined them. The last of the light had faded, but lamps had been hung in the trees, making the setting incredibly beautiful—the warmth of the late-spring night, the rippling of the river, the moon rising over the cliffs.

Incredibly romantic.

He should dance with someone else, he thought as they danced on. It was a bad thing only to dance with Rose. It went against everything she'd just warned him about. But she felt so…

So indescribable.

It was okay to dance with her, he told himself almost fiercely. She hadn't suggested changing partners. She wasn't wanting a relationship, so he could relax. He could marry her with no fear that she'd cling, and he could hold her right now, just as he was doing, without her fearing that he was making a move. He could savour the soft, yielding curves of her body. He could smell the citrusy fragrance of her hair.

He could…lose himself?

But he didn't. Of course he didn't. This was a weird interlude before reality raised its ugly head again—and here it was. Reality in the form of sirens, many sirens, the gentle lamplight overpowered by a score—maybe a hundred—vehicle lights.

Motorbikes and cars. A convoy.

Armed men.

The music and the dancing stopped. The men went swiftly to their horses, and the women ushered their children behind them, back to their individual modes of transport. Moving into protection mode.

A chauffeur climbed out of the leading car—a magnificent Rolls Royce—and ushered out its occupants. A man in a severe army-uniform. And a woman.

Julianna. There was enough about her to tell him this was Rose's sister, but where Rose looked what she was—a country vet—Julianna was a blonde beauty, a city sophisticate.

Rose was still held loosely in his arms. They were standing in the midst of the abandoned dance area. He felt her stiffen as Julianna appeared.

'It's Julianna,' she confirmed for his benefit only. 'I'd guess this must be Jacques.'

The big guns. The opposition.

'Let's do this optimistically,' he murmured into her hair. 'This is your sister. Go and tell her how exciting all this is. Don't pre-empt trouble by expecting it.'

But trouble was already with them. 'Julianna,'

Rose said, smiling, taking his advice and moving forward with her hands outstretched in greeting. She was forcing a warmth Nick knew she was far from feeling.

Julianna didn't smile. The woman was magnificently groomed, in cream linen-trousers, a cream silk-blouse mostly hidden by a luxurious fur jacket, and with magnificently groomed blonde hair caught into an elegant chignon. As Rose approached her, Julianna held out exquisitely manicured hands—not in welcome, but as if to ward her off.

'You're not welcome,' she said flatly, and Nick thought she sounded worried. Frightened, even. 'I don't want you here.'

'Erhard said we're very welcome,' Rose said, forcing her voice to stay light. 'He said this country is in trouble and Nick and I can help.'

'This is none of your business,' Julianna snapped. 'Our father didn't want you here, and neither do I. Jacques says you've entered the country illegally.'

'We entered this country on the royal jet.'

'Which was appropriated by unprivileged persons,' Julianna snapped. 'Jacques says you need to go back where you came from.'

'And me?' Nick asked, and stepped forward to hold Rose gently by the arm in a gesture that was as protective as it was proprietary.

Jacques moved then, holding his wife's arm in

a similar gesture to Nick's, but where Nick's hold was gentle there was a hint of underlying violence in Jacques' grip. He was a big man who looked accustomed to getting his own way, both within his own household and without.

'Enough,' Jacques said roughly. 'The succession is already decided, and any attempt by you to come here is seen as an attempt to undermine the throne. We tried to stop the flight, but Erhard...' He shrugged. 'No matter. His authority is at an end. My people will hold you in protective custody until we can arrange for your deportation.'

There was a shocked hush. The crowd drew a little bit closer, as if to better see what was happening. Two couples facing off—a big man in a uniform designed to intimidate, and his beautifully manicured wife. And Nick, without a tie, in the driver's borrowed jacket, flushed from dancing. Rose in her faded jeans and a soft cotton shirt that was threadbare from too many washes. Her hair escaping from her braid. A princess?

Deportation...

'You have no right to hold us in protective custody,' Nick said lightly, but with a hint of underlying strength. 'My papers are in order, as are those of Rose. There's no reason to hold us.'

'Hey, maybe it's just my sister's way of being polite,' Rose said, standing so close to him she seemed to be using his body as support.

'Julianna,' she said, forcing her voice to stay light. 'It's great to see you. Julianna's my sister,' she told the assemblage, as if she was proud of the fact. 'Does protective custody mean you're promising to look after us, Julianna?'

'I…' Julianna looked astounded. 'You…'

'You're taking us to the palace?' Rose asked.

'Would protective custody mean a palace?' Nick asked.

'It might,' Rose said. 'Protection doesn't mean dungeons.'

'There's dungeons in the palace,' someone called.

'Your sister surely wouldn't put us in a dungeon?' Nick said, forcing his words to sound lightly amused. 'That's hardly a family thing.'

'We're not a very close family,' Rose said, sounding dubious.

'Look, failing to send Christmas cards hardly deserves dungeons,' Nick said. 'Does it, Julianna?'

'I'm the Princess Julianna,' Julianna said, but she sounded worried.

'And I'm going to be your brother-in-law,' Nick said, sounding astonished. 'Surely we don't have to be formal in the family? You don't want to call your sister Princess Rose-Anitra, do you? Which you'd have to if we wanted to be formal, as she's just as much a princess as you are. Maybe even more as she's the Crown Princess.'

Whatever Julianna and Jacques had expected,

it wasn't this. The conversation included the crowd. There were cameras, and the journalist was taking furious notes. The journalist was backing into the crowd as she wrote, and the crowd was closing in around her, cutting her off from sight.

The photographer was still shooting, and there were a few other cameras in view as well. This was being documented, whether Jacques willed it or not.

And Jacques didn't like it one bit. 'This is a fiasco,' he yelled, staring round him in impotent fury.

'No, it's a picnic,' Rose said, clinging to Nick's hand proprietorially. 'These people have been really welcoming. But if you have other plans for us…'

'Take them,' Jacques growled, and the uniformed men moved in, surrounding them as if ready to seize them—or stop them escaping.

'Hey, we're coming, Julianna,' Rose said, still sounding amused. 'There's no need for your men to make an effort on our behalf. Coming, Nick? I think we're expected to go in that car.'

And before anyone could stop her she'd tugged Nick forward and slid into the Rolls Royce.

Nick slid in beside her. He was bemused, but his mind worked fast, and he was totally appreciative of what she'd done. With one swift movement she'd given Jacques and Julianna an invidious choice. They could haul Rose and Nick bodily from their car and toss them into one of the black cars that had been following—where they'd been clearly intended to go.

They could join them in the Rolls, intensifying the impression of family.

Or they could use one of the black cars themselves.

Nick sank into the soft leather of the Rolls, looked out and saw indecision on Jacques' face. And fury.

This was no game. They were playing for huge stakes here. Did Rose have any idea what she'd just done?

The stakes were upped about a millionfold. Jacques was being forced to state his case right now. Should he treat them as undignified prisoners, when Rose had just reminded the crowd that Julianna was her sister? Should he treat them as equals by climbing into the car with them? Or should he follow calmly behind?

Jacques looked apoplectic.

'Come,' Julianna said uncertainly, and tugged her husband forward towards the Rolls.

'No,' Jacques said, and sneered, slapping his wife's hand away. 'Let them go. Take them straight to the palace, as they said. Let them have their delusions of grandeur before they leave this place for ever.'

And he slammed the Rolls' door after Nick.

'Hoppy,' Rose said urgently, realising too late that her dog was still outside the car. 'Please… Hoppy!' she yelled.

'Take them away,' Jacques growled, and then, as Hoppy dived forward from where he'd been snoozing after a surfeit of sausages, Jacques drew back his booted leg and kicked him. Hard.

'Drive,' he yelled, and the car moved forward.

'You realise we're in trouble,' Nick said. They'd driven in silence for three minutes, and it seemed he was the first to have found his voice again.

'Hoppy's in trouble,' Rose whispered, sounding close to tears. 'He kicked him.'

'Yes, but he's okay.' He'd twisted and seen as they'd left the clearing. 'The little boy with the collie pup was picking him up.'

'He was alright?'

'Yes,' he said, although he couldn't be sure.

'He hates us,' Rose said in a small voice, and all the bravado had gone. All of a sudden she looked small and vulnerable, and…afraid? No, not afraid. Just sad. 'They both do. Julianna's my sister, and they both do.'

'I'm not sure that Julianna does. Jacques, yes, for what you represent.'

'Which is?'

'A threat to his future.'

'You think we should go home now?'

He smiled but it was a tiny smile. What had they got themselves into?

There was no friendly driver here. Their driver was in the same uniform as Jacques, albeit with less bars on his sleeve. He looked grim and businesslike, and there was no way they could talk to him through the sealed glass-partition.

The car was speeding northward into the city. Nick glanced behind them to see a stream of official cars. Black ones. There were outriders on motorcycles.

'Yorkshire's looking good,' he confessed, but at that Rose firmed and looked behind them and out at the outriders, and she set her face.

'No. No, it doesn't.'

'Hell, how bad was it?'

'You ever delivered a calf in a sleet storm in Yorkshire in February?'

'Um...no.'

'Dungeons are okay,' she said. She took a deep breath. 'They're a sight better than being a breeding mare.'

'A breeding mare?'

'Never mind,' she said flatly. 'That which doesn't kill us makes us stronger.'

'My foster mother used to say that about toothache,' he muttered. 'And I'm dead scared that what's in front of us isn't toothache.'

'Hey, you're not supposed to scare me,' she

said, still subdued but trying to sound indignant. 'You're the diplomat. Talk your way out of this.'

'I'm not exactly sure that's possible,' he said. 'I can't talk us out of this Rolls. Let's see where they put us next before we test my talking powers.'

She subsided back against the leather cushions. Her behavior back at the river had been brilliant, he thought. Yes, he was supposed to be the diplomat, but her diplomacy—and sheer effrontery in staring her sister and brother-in-law down—had been amazing.

But she was paying for it now. Reaction was starting to set in. Her face had paled, and when he glanced at her hands he saw she was clenching them together to stop them shaking.

He swore and moved across and tugged her against him.

She froze. 'We... We're not play-acting now,' she muttered.

'You mean I don't have to act like your husband? No,' he said grimly. 'But I do have to act like we're two people in trouble and I should have known something like this would happen.'

'How should you have known?'

'I'm a big boy. I just gave Erhard the benefit of the doubt—he said there wouldn't be major problems, and I—'

'Of course there would be major problems,'

she said, astounded. 'We're trying to wrest the throne.' Then she paused. 'But you aren't thinking major problems in the way I'm thinking major problems, are you? Major problems to me are being escorted to the airport and told to leave.'

'I guess there are more major problems than that.'

'Like imprisonment.'

'Yes.'

She didn't relax, but he felt her body edge closer to his, gaining comfort in the nearness of him. As indeed he was gaining comfort from her.

'You think someone will look after Hoppy?' she whispered in a small voice.

'Of course they will.'

'Not Jacques' men.'

'No, but there were people sympathetic to our cause. I'm sure they'll take care of him.'

'But he's been kicked.'

'He'll be okay,' he muttered, and found his fingers had clenched into fists. To kick this woman's dog…

And his reaction was for Hoppy too, he thought with a start. How had that happened?

Early in life Nick had learned to be independent. His foster brothers were like him—taught early to be loners. Ruby, their foster mother, had done everything in her power to teach them to love, and maybe they did love her. But to extend that loving…

Nick had never really thought of it until he'd met Rose, and here he was realising that after only hours' acquaintance he'd go to quite some trouble to make sure Hoppy was safe. For Hoppy's sake. Just for the way the dumb dog had wriggled his tail in ecstasy when dinner had arrived on the plane. Then, as he'd realised the two plates were meant for Rose and Nick, he'd transformed, crouching low on his haunches, covering his nose with his front paws and then looking mournfully over—a lost orphan dog who no one had fed for the last month but far too polite to ask… Until Griswold had brought him his own steak.

'You're smiling,' Rose said, staring at him, and he brought himself back to the present with a start. They were being hauled off to goodness knew where and he was thinking about a dog.

'I was thinking that if anyone can survive Hoppy will.'

'Yeah,' she agreed, and managed a rueful smile in return. 'I guess.'

'I'm sure of it.'

'You think maybe we should worry about us first?'

'Maybe it'd be sensible.' She was huddled against him and he welcomed her warmth. He wanted to hug her closer, hold her tight, but he wasn't sure how she'd take it. He thought back to the words she'd spoken while they'd been dancing. *No more relationships.*

Like him. So they were fine.

'So you're thinking, maybe, firing squad at dawn?' she asked, in a tone that said she suspected the direction his thoughts were taking and it was time he got back to matters of import. Like firing squads. Right.

But at least he could reassure her there. 'Rose, they can't,' he said, quelling the sudden urge to kiss her lightly—just as a reassurance. But she was withdrawing, moving slightly away from him as she regained control, and so must he.

'These people aren't criminals,' he told her. 'The people in charge here are out for their own gain, but to bankrupt the country and leave themselves nowhere to run would defeat their purpose. Every member of the Council has homes in places like the south of France, or Capri or, well, places where they can enjoy swanning round with their wealth. If we were to disappear without trace, they'd be international criminals.'

She thought that through. 'You checked?'

'I checked,' he said. 'And I do work for a huge international law-firm. I'm not too keen on the assassination bit, but opinion was unanimous that we'd be safe. So let's not worry, and see where they take us.'

'To the palace?' she said, trying to sound hopeful.

'Five-star luxury coming up,' he said, and grinned. 'Let's count on it.'

CHAPTER SEVEN

THEY were indeed going to the palace. The car pulled up in the forecourt of a building that brought Rose's memories flooding back. The grand palace of the royal family of Alp de Montez.

'I'd forgotten it was so grand,' Rose whispered, staring up at gleaming white turrets, battlements, fountains in the forecourt two stories high, marble steps leading to an entrance that took up an area the size of a tennis court. 'My mother was never given an independent allowance. So here we stayed. I was tutored here, and we hardly left the place. But I'd forgotten…'

It looked like something out of a fairy tale. Could she really be a princess?

And then the car door was hauled open by men in uniform, and the fairy tale evaporated like the bursting of a bubble.

'Out,' someone snapped, and a hand grabbed her arm and tugged so hard she fell out onto the gravel.

But she had a protector. In seconds Nick was

on her side of the car, lifting her to her feet, pushing the uniformed thugs aside as if it was he who was in charge and not these people. He set Rose firmly before him, and placed a hand strongly on each shoulder. He smiled at her, a 'we're in this together' smile. And then he faced Jacques. The black car that had drawn up right behind them had disgorged Jacques and his lady. Julianna.

'If you lay a finger on the Princess Rose, you'll be facing enquiries from the international community,' Nick said in a carrying, commanding voice he must have perfected in years of work as a lawyer. Now he deepened his voice, making it louder, as if wanting to carry his words as far as possible.

'Princess Rose-Anitra and I—Nikolai de Montez—have been escorted to the Imperial Castle of Alp de Montez against our will,' he said strongly, loudly, to the world at large. 'The date is… The time is… We're being held in custody by Jacques and Julianna de Montez. Jacques and Julianna are here right now, in my sight, with direct authority over the people holding us.'

What was he doing?

'At any moment my mobile phone will be taken from me,' he continued. 'I will then stop transmitting, but this message is recorded. Blake, you know what to do.'

There was a moment's taut stillness—and then a roar of fury from Jacques as he realised what Nick had just done. The man who'd done the talking back at the river and at the airport—Dupeaux—snapped a curt order. Nick was summarily searched and a mobile phone tugged from his shirt pocket.

'It's still transmitting,' Nick said blandly as Dupeaux handed it to Jacques. Again he raised his voice. 'The phone's been forcibly removed from me.'

Jacques threw the phone on the ground and ground it with his heel.

'I'd guess it's stopped transmitting now,' Nick said and smiled, tugging Rose tight against him. 'But it's been transmitting to my foster brother, Blake, partner in the international law-firm Goodman, Stern and Haddock. I commenced recording back at the river, and what I just said has been transmitted as well. If Blake—and my friends at almost every international embassy in London—don't hear from us soon they'll know where to look. Wouldn't you say?'

He smiled again. But Jacques wasn't smiling.

'Take them away,' he snapped, staring down at the ruined phone as if it was a live scorpion.

But… Julianna?

'Julianna?' Rose asked, turning to her sister. Julianna seemed almost stunned with what was happening. Surely the transmission thing hadn't been necessary. Surely in this day and age…

'You're threatening us,' Julianna whispered, and her face was white with shock.

'You're threatening this country,' Rose said.

'We're not. Jacques isn't.'

'Ask the hard questions, Julia,' Rose told her, but she had to yell her last two words over her shoulder. They were being hustled away.

To…a dungeon?

Not quite.

They passed through three thick doors, hustled so fast they hardly had time to be aware of their surroundings. Then they were unceremoniously shoved through a final door, and the clang of metal against stone echoed solidly as they were left alone.

Breathless with shock, Rose stared around her in dismay. By this time she'd almost been expecting to see a torture chamber. She'd never seen such a thing when she was a child, but circumstances now made her fear the worst.

It wasn't a dungeon. Not even close. It was an austere room, whitewashed with a concrete floor, and she recognised it as one of a number of windowless storerooms under the castle. Two single beds were simply made with white coverlets. A small, wool mat lay between each bed, a solitary concession to comfort. Through a door on the other side of the room she could see simple bathroom facilities.

Austere, but not scary.

'So much for me wanting to be a princess with tiaras and everything,' she whispered, and she couldn't keep her voice steady.

'Rose…'

'It's alright. It's still better than Yorkshire.'

Nick was right. This was her choice, she told herself. There'd had to be some imperative to give her the moral strength to walk away from Max's life. Well, this was surely a moral imperative. And a physical imperative. She couldn't return if she tried.

She touched the door, tentatively, putting pressure on the handle.

'It's locked,' Nick said unnecessarily.

'I guessed.'

'Hell, Rose…'

'It's okay,' she whispered.

'Would you mind very much if I hugged you?' Nick asked.

'I…'

'You see, I don't much like enclosed places,' he confessed. 'I think I'm claustrophobic.'

'You think?'

'I need a hug,' he said, and he turned and took her into his arms.

He was claustrophobic?

She didn't believe it for a minute. He was just saying it because he thought she needed a hug herself.

He was absolutely right. This was deeply, deeply scary. And where, *where*, was Hoppy?

She let herself be drawn against him. Again. She was getting almost accustomed to it, she thought as she let him tug her into his arms, and then she forgot to think.

He needed a hug to drive away fear? Well, maybe he was right at that, for a hug from this man did drive away fear. It drove away everything. The strength of him, the sheer arrant maleness of him… This man had a reputation as a womaniser and she was starting to see why. What woman wouldn't react to Nikolai de Montez exactly as she was reacting now?

He was gorgeous. And she was afraid. For all her bravado, for all his assurances of her long-term safety, she'd seen the look on Jacques' face, and it had been hatred. She was being held a prisoner.

She'd lost Hoppy.

The last was the worst. She shuddered and he tugged her closer, his fingers raking her hair with gentle reassurance.

'Hey, it's okay. It's okay, Rose. This is just a hiccup. We'll get out of here, you'll see.'

'It's you who's supposed to be afraid,' she

retorted, but she didn't pull away. Not when he was raking her hair, just as it should be raked.

'Someone will take care of Hoppy,' he said, and she froze against him.

'I'm a vet,' she whispered into the muffling anonymity of his shoulder. 'Hoppy's had a couple of his lives already. I shouldn't care so much.'

'If you didn't care so much you wouldn't be you,' he told her. 'Did you have to stay with your in-laws for so long?'

She frowned, but she was frowning against the warmth and strength of his shoulder. She had no intention of pulling away just yet.

'What's that got to do with the price of fish?' she managed, and she felt rather than saw him smile.

'Nothing. But we're in prison. We might as well fill the time socially.'

'By cuddling.'

'And talking,' he said gravely. 'Saving me from claustrophobia.'

'You're not really claustrophobic.'

'Let go of me and I'll start climbing walls. And hollering. You want to see a grown man turn into a caged animal?'

She smiled, but she did manage to pull away. Just a little.

A lock of his hair had fallen over his eyes. He did look anxious. But there was a hint of laughter behind his dark eyes that belied the anxiety he was expressing. This man was dangerous, she told herself. This whole situation was dangerous, but the most dangerous thing of all was that she was locked in a single cell with Nick.

'You're on your own,' she said, broke away and went to sit on the far bunk. She sat with the expectation that there'd be a bit of spring in the bed. There wasn't. Her backside hit with a solid thud.

'Ouch!' Nick said, seeing the way her body reacted.

'Hard as nails.' Then as he made to sit beside her she slid along further so the area he'd attempted to sit on was blocked. 'Bounce on your own bed.'

'What fun is that?'

'There isn't any fun in what's happening.'

'Let's assume there is,' he said. He sat down on the other bed, seemingly obedient, and smiled at her with a smile that wasn't the least bit obedient. 'Just to stop me being claustrophobic.'

'Cut it out with the claustrophobia,' she told him.

'Telling someone to cut it out isn't exactly a tried and true therapeutic approach to the problem. Whereas my idea—distraction—is much more likely to work.'

'So how long do you think they'll keep us here?' she demanded, and he shrugged.

'This is unknown territory, Rose.' His voice

was suddenly serious. 'But we've done all we can. We've presented our case to as many people as we could. As long as that message isn't able to be suppressed, then things will happen. Erhard said this country has been suppressed for so long that it's a powder keg waiting to blow.'

'With us in the middle.'

'No, because we're an alternative to blowing,' he said, still serious. 'The people here don't want anarchy—you just have to look at how long they've put up with dreadful rulers to see that. So with us they don't have to change the status quo. All they have to do is insist on the application of the law.'

'So how are they going to do that—ask Julianna and Jacques politely to let us take over?'

'I have no idea.'

'You've gone into this as blindly as I have.'

'Maybe not quite,' he admitted. 'I did have the reassurance of almost everyone else on the staff. And my brother.'

'Your brother,' she said, thinking things through and not able to work it out.'

'I have six foster-brothers,' he told her. 'One of whom is Blake, who's in the same law firm as I am. He was on the other end of the telephone. "If in doubt, ring and I'll record"—that's what he told me as we left. I did. So everything we've said since we landed has been recorded.'

'So Blake will come with a battalion of armed SAS agents.'

'It won't come to that.'

'Are you sure?'

'No,' he admitted.

'And Blake doesn't have an army, does he?'

'Um, no.'

'And my dog's wandering the country, friendless.'

'He won't be.'

'I think I'm going to bed,' she said, giving her hard bed another tentative poke. 'My conversation with you is getting me nowhere.'

'You'll sleep?'

'It's almost midnight,' she said. 'So maybe I will. You don't think if we asked nicely they might give us our luggage?'

'Um…'

'You don't know that either,' she said, and sighed. And then brightened. 'Hey, but I'm set.'

'You're set?'

She tugged off her duffel coat and foraged in an inner pocket, then triumphantly produced a battered-looking toothbrush and a half-empty tube of toothpaste. She held it up like it was the crown jewels.

'Bet high-flying lawyers don't carry toothpaste on their persons,' she said smugly.

'Um…no. Can I ask why?'

'I keep getting stuck,' she told him. 'I'll go to a calving and it'll be four in the morning, and as I finish the farmer will say can I hang around until his pig farrows or his neighbour's cow calves. It's too far to go home, so I kip on the couch and keep going. Hence the toothpaste.' She smiled. 'I'll lend you toothpaste, but you'll have to use your finger cos I'm not sharing toothbrushes. Even if we are going to be married, which I'm starting to seriously doubt.'

And she smiled, took herself to the bathroom and closed the door behind her.

She slept.

He was quite frankly astonished. To have the ability to close her eyes and sleep... It was a gift.

He wished he had it. Even as a kid he'd never been able to sleep. Bad things happened when you slept...

Where had that come from? The weird background of his past, where his mother was a shadowy figure moving in and out as life's events lurched around her.

'She was a frightened kid,' Ruby had told him when he was old enough to respond to his foster mother's deep concerns about his nightmares—where people had come and gone in the dark, and sometimes his mother had wept, sometimes she'd disappeared with the shadows, and when he'd woken she wasn't there. 'Your mother had nightmares of her own,' Ruby had told him. 'They didn't let her grow up properly. The trick is—the thing we have to do—is to take charge of your nightmares and see if we can find you a way to live through them.'

She was a wise woman, Ruby. His one true thing. He and his six foster-brothers had been blessed by her taking charge of their shattered lives.

Ruby had been sensible enough to know he could never escape completely from the nightmares. Just learn to live around them.

So, dredging up a Ruby lesson from the past, he didn't try to sleep now. He lay and watched the ceiling as he'd lain and watched the ceiling, countless nights in his past, not trying to sleep, just letting his thoughts go where they would.

But the ceiling wasn't interesting. There was a light on through the other side of their prison's thick doors, and he could see faintly by the chink of light it permitted in.

He could watch Rose.

Brave, he thought. Brave and lonely. But so practical. So accustomed to moving through grief.

She'd lost her dog this day. He knew already how much Hoppy meant to her, but had she wept or made a fuss?

There was nothing she could do about it. He'd been watching her eyes as she'd spoken of Hoppy and he knew how much it had hurt, how much she'd wanted to be out looking.

But there was nothing to be done, so a fuss hadn't been made. There was nothing to do, so she'd settled for sleep.

She was some woman. A woman in a million. Like Ruby.

Ruby would love her, he thought, and then thought maybe, just maybe, he should have told Ruby more of what was happening. He'd described this marriage to his foster mother as a political move, nothing more. She'd been horrified, for she wanted so much more for her beloved sons.

Maybe Ruby was wiser than he was, he thought ruefully, for there was nothing political about how he was thinking of Rose.

He watched on. An hour. Two. This place was cold. They'd been given one blanket each. He was still wearing all his clothes, bar his shoes. The room was chill and getting colder.

'I'm cold,' Rose said into the silence, and he jumped about a foot.

'I thought you were asleep.'

'I was,' she said. 'But I just woke up. One blanket isn't going to cut it.'

'You've got your duffel coat.'

'I have,' she agreed equably. 'So my top half is cosy. My bottom half is jealous. Do you only have one blanket?'

'I… Yes.'

'Could I trust you if I said you were welcome to share my bed?'

That took his breath away. 'You're proposing we sleep together?' he asked cautiously.

'Not in the metaphoric sense,' she said lightly. 'In the literal sense.'

'You mean sleep as in *sleep*.'

'Take it or leave it,' she said. 'It's a once-in-a-lifetime offer.'

'Never knock a lady back,' he said, and two seconds later he was spreading his blanket over her and then diving under the covers as well.

'I have another suggestion,' she said before he could attempt to settle.

'Which is?'

'My feet are freezing,' she said. 'We've both got jackets on. If I spread my nice woolly duffel over our feet, you could put our limousine driver's jacket over our tops. Note that this is a major concession on my part,' she said before he could move. 'Because my duffel is very, very warm, and your leather jacket won't be nearly as warm, not to mention that it's really been lent to both of us. So I could be within my rights to keep my duffel just for me, but insist that your leather jacket goes over our feet. But I'm magnanimous,' she said in a truly magnanimous voice.

He chuckled.

They spent a convivial couple of minutes arranging their bed. Two blankets. The duffel spread-eagled over the bottom half. The leather jacket over the top. Then they were both under.

She was in her jeans and a cotton shirt. He was in his trousers and linen shirt. His tie was still in his pocket.

Sleeping in her jeans would be uncomfortable. They now had sufficient coverings that taking off their outer clothes would be sensible, but he wasn't about to suggest it.

The bed was too narrow for them to lie apart. Their bodies touched, side by side. He lay rigid.

This was impossible. They were two mature people, and…

'This is crazy,' she said. 'We're never going to sleep like this.'

'So what do you suppose we do about it?'

'Relax,' she said. 'If I lie on my side and you lie on the same side, you'll curve round me and keep me warm. I'm a widow. I know.'

'I…I guess,' he said doubtfully, trying to figure how this could stay a nice, platonic sharing of beds—and she was *so* close.

'And you're not a widower, but I'm betting you know as well that people can sleep together without wanting sex,' she said. 'So stop lying there like you're standing at attention, only lying down. Relax.'

'Yes, ma'am.'

'That's better,' she said, and he felt rather than saw her smile as she turned on her side, waited patiently for him to do the same and then wriggled until her spine was curved against his chest.

Unbidden, his arms came round to hold her.

She stiffened—just for a moment—and then she relaxed again.

'See, it's not just me coming up with the ideas,' she said. 'Excellent. Now, relax and go to sleep. Unless you're worried about being taken out at dawn and shot. But we have Blake to stop that happening, right?'

'Um, right.'

'Then what else is there to worry about?' she said. 'Apart from Hoppy, and there's nothing I can do about him until they let us out of here. So we might as well sleep. Sleep!'

'Yes, ma'am.'

And he did. He closed his eyes, and when he opened them again to his unutterable astonishment he'd slept for hours.

Rose was still deeply asleep, curled against his breast as if she belonged there. He was still holding her, his left arm underneath her, tugging her tight against him even in sleep. His right arm was resting lightly on her shoulder. He had to move slightly to see his watch, but she didn't stir.

She must have been exhausted, he thought. Damn, he should have researched her background further. He wanted to know…

He did know.

He'd never lain with a woman like this. Never. She felt different, amazing, exciting…warm, and…as if she belonged.

She did belong, he thought, with a sure knowledge starting deep within. It had started that first night he'd met her, and it had grown deeper last night as he'd watched her work the crowd with an intuitive empathy he'd never seen in his years of working in the international legal community. Then last night, tossed into prison with a man she hardly knew, losing a dog she obviously loved deeply, thrown into an uncertain future…

She'd been brave beyond belief. She'd been upbeat and courageous, laughing whenever she could, refusing to be intimidated, treating the situation as something to be faced with optimism.

She stirred a fraction in his arms and his hold on her tightened.

This woman was affianced to be his wife, he thought with something approaching incredulity. His wife.

In name only.

But now things had changed. What was inside him had changed.

Had he fallen in love?

The thought was so startling that he must have moved or gasped—or maybe she could feel the sheer force of what he was thinking. She lay motionless in his arms, but he could feel that she was awake.

He didn't speak, letting her make the first move. If she wanted to wake up slowly, well, she'd earned the right. She'd earned the right to do whatever she wanted, he thought. Rose…

'What's the time?' she whispered, and he knew she didn't want this time to stop.

'Seven.'

'Do you think they'll feed us?'

As if on cue the door swung open. A tray was put on the floor and shoved forward, and the door was slammed shut before they could see who their jailer was.

'I guess the answer to that is yes,' he said, and as she stirred he reluctantly released her and sat up. It was unbelievable what he was feeling about her right now. His world had changed.

'Don't look like that,' she said, suddenly getting businesslike, sliding to the end of the bed so she could get out without pushing past him.

'Like what?'

'I don't know. I don't know what you're thinking, and I don't intend to ask,' she said briskly. 'I bags the bathroom first, and don't you dare eat all the toast.'

There wasn't toast. There was cereal and long-life milk, tepid water and instant coffee.

'Not what I had in mind when I decided to be a princess again,' Rose muttered. 'Is this a good time to tell you I'm addicted to good coffee and if I'm deprived I'm scary?'

'Me too,' Nick said.

'So what do we do now?' Rose asked, finishing her coffee resolutely, even though wrinkling her nose in distaste.

'I guess we wait.'

'How long do you reckon?'

'Twenty years?'

'They'll have to give us a pack of cards, then,' Rose said, seemingly unperturbed. 'Otherwise I'll write a letter to the United Nations.'

He smiled. Things firmed even further.

They sat down to wait.

If anyone had told Rose that she'd tell her complete life story to a man she'd met once almost a month ago, she would have said they were crazy. Nuts. She wasn't an extrovert. She'd married Max, but even Max had needed time to coax her out of her shell. Finally she'd learned to trust him, but that trust had landed her into a mess over her head. Her privacy had become the shared concern of Max's family. Everything she told him his family had known too, as well as the whole village. So she'd learned once more to shut up.

Yet here she was, handing out private information like it was free.

Why? Maybe it was because Nick didn't really want it, she told herself. He was asking because he was bored and there was nothing else to do. When this whole fiasco was over, no matter how it ended, he'd head back to his city law-firm and she'd be isolated, just as she desperately wanted.

So he was asking questions, and there was no pack of cards, and she didn't want to spend time thinking about all the various fates in store for someone who tried to take the crown—so what was a girl to do, but answer his questions honestly and ask questions herself and pretend to be interested in the answers?

Actually she *was* interested, and that was the problem. It was a little like a game of snap, she thought. They'd both had bleak childhoods—their legacy from their connection to this ill-fated royal family. They'd learned to be independent, which was only a tiny factor in their shared passions.

'Do you play tennis?'

'No, but I love hockey. I was hopeless, as I didn't play until I got to England, but I love it now. I still play. Or, until last week I played.'

'You're kidding. I played hockey for my university.'

'Forward?'

'Centre-forward mostly. You?'

'Mostly right full-forward,' she said. 'I hit harder to the left.'

'If we had a couple of sticks now we could have a battle.'

'If we're stuck in this place much longer we could pull the bed apart and use the planks,' she said. 'So let's delay the hockey match till tomorrow. Meanwhile, what about ice cream? What's your favourite flavour?'

'I'm a chocolate man.'

'With choc chips?'

'Ugh, no. I like my chocolate melted in, triple or quadruple-strength chocolate, and no crunchy bits to deflect the taste.'

'Yum,' she said, feeling suddenly hungry. 'When do you reckon lunch will arrive?'

'I think our chances of ice cream for lunch are minimal. What about swimming?'

'Five strokes and then I go under,' she said. 'This place never ran to a swimming pool. Maybe it has one now. Here's hoping. What about you?'

'My foster mother's cottage just outside Sydney had a dam in the back paddock. We all had to learn to swim across it before we were allowed out of Ruby's sight.'

'So Ruby taught you?'

'Ruby taught me everything.'

'Lucky you,' she said.

'For having a foster mother?'

'I…I guess. Sorry. Dumb comment.'

'No, it's okay. But you—when we get to live in this luxurious palace with an Olympic-sized swimming pool…'

'Then we buy me some floaties and don't let photographers near. Nick, what do you think is happening outside?'

'I don't know.'

They'd been aware of the noise since just after breakfast. At first it had sounded like a faint far-off rumble, as if maybe they were not too far away from a sports pavilion. It wasn't so much individual sound—more a steady murmur, slowly building. But it was building. In the last few minutes it had become so close they could hear individual voices.

'It's well over time for lunch,' she said nervously. 'Maybe we should complain.'

'Let's not,' Nick said. 'I have a feeling whoever's on lunch duty might be distracted.'

They listened for a while longer. The shouts became louder. Whoever it was, they weren't going away.

'How are you at singing?' Nick asked, and Rose thought about singing and then thought, no, this sound was getting too loud to permit distraction. It was definitely loud. It was definitely close.

'You know, if this is a revolution, the age-old way to depose monarchy is to do a bit of head chopping,' she whispered.

'The Russians were the last,' he said, obviously distracted too. 'But royalty's been ousted efficiently since, with nary a bruised neck to show for it. Look at the women's magazines. There are prince and princesses all over the place, minus thrones, but necks nicely intact.'

'Nick…'

'I know,' he said. He'd crossed to the door, trying hard to hear individual noises from the background din. But there'd been need in her voice. She'd heard it, but there wasn't anything she could do about it.

This was supposed to be an adventure. How could it suddenly have got so serious? And where was Julianna? Her sister.

And Hoppy…

'Nick,' she said again, not even trying to disguise her need this time. And he reacted. In three long strides he'd crossed the room and hugged her close.

'We're in this together,' he whispered, and his lips brushed the top of her hair.

That should make her feel safer. It did—sort of. It made her feel as if she could face anything with his arms around her for support, but that was scary all by itself. The feeling that she was starting to depend on him.

This man was an international businessman—

a jet-setter who'd agreed to a marriage of convenience.

What had she done? A normal woman would have listened to Erhard's proposition and treated him like a very polite madman. To leave her home and come halfway across Europe to claim a throne—to threaten her sister, to involve herself in a power struggle where she had no idea who the players were, much less how to deal with them... It was like she'd stepped into a James Bond movie, but it was real.

She'd guessed there'd be risks. At some subliminal level she'd figured that this couldn't be as easy as Erhard had suggested—arrive here, say 'move over' to Julianna, and become a princess. Yet things had been closing in on her so tightly at home that she'd come regardless. And the really frightening thing now was that although she should be terrified of outside factors—like a crowd of what sounded like thousands gathering in the castle surrounds—she hugged tight to this man and she still thought that it was okay. Better to go down fighting with this man by her side than to stay for ever in Yorkshire and keep calmly on living Max's life.

'We're in this together,' he whispered into her hair, and that was terrifying as well. She'd have to do something about it. He was holding her as if he loved her.

As if he loved her...

She hadn't slashed one set of silver chains to be caught by another, she told herself fiercely. No more emotional baggage. Ever.

Except right now she couldn't pull away from Nick's arms. Right now she lacked the strength to be independent, so she held on while the noise from outside grew to an ear-shattering roar. There was a sudden burst of gunfire, and that made her cling tighter, and it made Nick hold her closer. What was happening—a revolution outside their prison door? What? *What?*

The gunfire stopped as abruptly as it had started. There was a sudden lull, and then a vast, roaring cheer of approval.

It went on and on, but finally it grew muted. The roar subsided and sounds of confusion took its place. People yelling. Individual voices growing closer.

Was this what war was like? Rose had stopped thinking about how close she was holding Nick. If he tried to pull away now she'd fight him. And by the feel of his arms he was feeling exactly the same as she was.

The shouts grew louder. People yelling to each other. Jubilant yells. But why jubilant?

They stared at the locked door as if it was a time bomb. The minutes ticked by.

And then a shout of approval from just through

the door. Men's voices, shouting, demanding. The sound of a key in the lock.

The door swung inward, and a crowd of people stood in the doorway.

Facing them was the earnest young reporter who'd interviewed them the night before. Behind her was the cameraman, his camera raised over his head, flash flaring.

And pushing through was a child—the boy with the scraggy collie from the night before. There was a man holding the child by the shoulders, trying to make him stay back a little, but he was still pushing through.

'Let him through,' the man said earnestly as the door swung wider still and people started surging in. 'The boy has the lady's dog.' He pushed hard, the reporter gave way and the child burst into the room.

He was holding out Hoppy. Rose gasped. And then she smiled.

'Hoppy!' she said, and knelt and held out her arms. 'Oh, Hoppy. I might have known I'd be rescued by a dog.'

CHAPTER EIGHT

HER wedding day dawned as the day most brides dream of. It was a perfect spring day. When the maid pushed back the drapes, she turned to Rose and she beamed her approval.

'Happy is the bride who the sun shines on.'

'Yeah?' Rose groaned and thrust back her covers. Revealing Hoppy. This was a huge and scary palace, and Hoppy had decided his mistress needed round the clock protection.

There really was no need of it. The murmurings of dissent had grown to a full-throated roar the night of their arrival. The population had arrived at the castle to voice their dissent. Hundreds had turned to thousands. There'd been one burst of gunfire over the head of the crowd, to try and stem the rush, but they'd still kept coming.

Jacques and Julianna had disappeared, their heavies with them, only agreeing because they were forced to that the succession be decided by the international panel. The panel had yet to meet, but there seemed little chance that Erhard would be proved wrong. As long as this marriage took place, the throne would go to Rose.

Was it too good to be true? Maybe. Rose was still uneasy, as was Nick, but there was nothing that could be done but continue what they'd planned.

A wedding. Today.

'Prince Nikolai breakfasted before you, ma'am,' the maid said, beaming romantically. 'For a groom to see the bride before the ceremony is bad luck.'

Well, we wouldn't want that, Rose thought. Not now.

For this was going exactly as planned. Nick would marry her today. The succession would be organized. Nick would be free to leave her, and return to his career.

So why wasn't she happy?

It was just… Well, living happily ever after as reigning sovereign was starting to feel a bit empty. What would she do?

'The hairdresser will be here in an hour,' the maid told her. 'And your dress will be ready at twelve. Photographers at two.'

See, that was the problem. She hadn't factored in the 'princess' stuff.

Nothing to do but reign.

Without Nick.

Her mother had been a royal bride, and she'd been isolated for ever. Was that what she was condemning herself to?

Yeah, but… *Yeah, but…*

'I wanted to be by myself,' she told Hoppy as the maid left, but Hoppy gave her a quizzical look, leaped off the bed and trotted to the bedroom door. They'd been here only a week, but already Hoppy knew and approved of her routine. Breakfast with Nick. A couple of hours in the office working through the reams of paperwork, trying to get her head around stuff that Nick understood better than she did. But he wouldn't be here for ever to help her. Then maybe a long hike in the woods. With Nick. A swim with Nick—yes, as the old Prince had lost authority his son had installed a pool. A magnificent pool. Nick was teaching her, and already she could dog-paddle.

Then maybe a picnic.

Then dinner and conversation long into the night. And then…

Bed alone.

He is going to be your husband. A little voice had been saying that over and over to her in the past week. It wouldn't hurt to…

But it would hurt.

'I'm getting the happy-ever-after without the prince,' Rose told her dog, firmly stifling the doubts. 'And the last step I have to take before I can start my happy-ever-after is to marry.'

So get on with it.

He stood alone at the end of the aisle of the palace chapel. This chapel was no grand architectural statement. Unlike the rest of the palace it had been built with love—making it a place where humans could seek sanctuary from troubles surrounding them. It seemed almost intimate. Apart from the crowd of dignitaries filling the chapel to almost bursting. And the television camera broadcasting their union to the world.

Rose entered the church—and she paused.

Up until now it had seemed a dream. An escape. She'd been running from a situation that had threatened to overwhelm her. From the time she'd walked in to the restaurant five weeks ago things had moved in fast motion, a blur of things that had had to be done. Organisation. The chaos of arriving here. The fuss associated with this royal wedding.

This dress alone; the royal dressmakers had spent hour upon hour with the heirloom wedding gown, altering the fragile lace, fitting it so that it seemed like a second skin. The people wanted a fuss. The people were desperate for a royal bride. That's what she'd been told over and over since she and Nick had been let out of their underground prison.

'The news that you are here has inspired the country as nothing else could. A clean sweep without bloodshed—oh, my dear, how wonderful. And you and Prince Nikolai… You're such a romantic couple. There won't be a dry eye in the country.'

She'd blocked that comment, expressed by the chief dressmaker but seemingly echoing the sentiments of the populace. But now, as the organ was swelling into the first chords of the bridal march, she paused and took a breath.

What was she doing?

The last time she'd heard this music, she'd been in a tiny church in Yorkshire and Max had been waiting for her.

Now Nick was waiting for her. The whole sweet trap.

And it rose up to catch her. She caught her breath in panic. Her feet refused to move.

Nick was at the end of the aisle, but he was a blur, seen through misting eyes, too far away to see her panic, too far away to help.

An elderly man rose from the pew beside the door. He placed a hand on her arm, and she turned in shock.

Erhard.

She hadn't seen him for five weeks. She'd been told he was convalescing from illness. He'd made a couple of organisational phone calls but he'd stayed away. She and Nick had both worried, but he'd refused to let them see him.

For him to be here now seemed almost magic.

He'd shrunk a little, but in other ways he'd expanded. He was wearing full military uniform. Tassels and braid everywhere. A dress sword. And he was smiling.

'Nikolai isn't the same as Max,' he said softly, and his grip on her arm was surprisingly strong. 'You know that.'

She looked into his face for a minute and he met her look, unflinching. How had he known?

'He's waiting for you,' he said.

She turned to look towards Nick. Panic cleared.

Nick was concerned. She could see that even from here. He was watching, waiting, but there was a slight furrow in his brow that said he knew she was troubled.

How did he know that? How could he tell that from here? And how could she know that he knew?

He looked fabulous. He was wearing the same uniform as Erhard, rich, deep, deep blue, with red and gold braid, tassels, a golden sash slashing across his chest, and a dress sword hung by his side.

Nikolai de Montez. A prince coming home. He looked the part.

He should be sovereign and not me, she thought, starting to feel hysterical. He looked fabulous. He looked royal. He looked so far apart from her world that she felt giddy.

The whole chapel was waiting for her to start walking. To go to her bridegroom. But Erhard's pressure on her arm wasn't insistent—he was waiting for her to decide. Letting her take her time.

Nikolai was waiting.

And then Nick smiled. He stooped and lifted something from the floor.

Hoppy.

She'd left Hoppy in the care of one of the palace gardeners. The little dog had made friends of everyone here, so much so that Nick had suggested the reason for the country's insurrection was that Jacques had kicked the dog. It was a tiny thing in the scheme of things, but it had been caught on camera, and Jacques had not been seen in public since. Hoppy, however, had been in demand. For every photo call there had been the request: 'and the little dog?'

Rose had thought he had no place here today in this most formal of ceremonies. But Nick obviously had had other ideas.

The furrow of worry had disappeared from Nick's brow. He was smiling. Hoppy was tucked under his arm, and then, maybe lest she thought it was some sort of enticement for her to come to him, Nick set the little dog on his three feet.

He'd been washed and brushed until he shone. He looked almost regal. There was a gold and blue riband stretched around his chest, matching Nick's to perfection.

He waved his tail like a flag, seemingly aware that the eyes of the world were upon him, lapping up the attention.

'Go to Rose,' Nick said.

The bridal march was still playing. Hoppy looked up at Nick enquiringly, then gazed around the church while all the dignitaries, officials and palace staff held their collective breath.

Hoppy had watched her dress. He knew that this confection of white-and-cream lace and ribbon was his mistress. His disreputable tail gave another happy wag and he set off down the aisle at full tilt.

Hop-along Hoppy.

Rose giggled and bent down to greet him. Hoppy reached her and bounded up into her arms, wriggling all over. She gathered him to her, then straightened and looked ahead at Nick. He was still smiling.

And suddenly this was as far as it was possible to be from that long-ago wedding to Max. She remembered it—the tiny church in Yorkshire, Max waiting looking thin and gaunt and anxious, and his parents sitting by him, fretting that everything was as it should be.

The bride's guests sat on the left, the groom's on the right. That was the way it should be, and Max's mother had strictly enforced it. 'Are you Max's friend?' she'd directed the ushers to ask, and if the friend said yes, regardless of the fact that she and Max shared many friends, then they'd been directed to the right as well.

So she'd walked into the church and there'd been three lone stragglers, friends who'd defied her mother-in-law's rules and sat on her side regardless.

It had been Max's wedding. It had been nothing to do with her.

It had been Max's life.

But here both sides of the church were crowded, even if it was with strangers. Erhard was beside her, calmly smiling, giving her all the time in the world. Hoppy was trying to lick her face.

Nick was smiling.

This was *her* life. That flash of certainty she'd had when Erhard had first put this proposition to her, when she'd sat across the dinner table from Nick and looked at the way he'd talked to Erhard, courteous, kind, sensitive...

There were no strings here. This was no golden net waiting to catch her, hold her, as it had held her mother. Nick was doing this to free this country. Sure he'd kissed and held her, and he'd been her rock during the past few days, but there were no conditions.

She could marry him and he'd walk away and leave her to it.

He was watching her, hopeful but uncertain. The whole church was watching her uncertainly. What was she doing? Having second thoughts in front of the world's press? Giving Erhard and Nick heart attacks? If Julianna and Jacques were watching her now they'd beam with delight. Or say really loudly to the nation, *see, she's vacillating*.

It was only the thought of marriage that had her vacillating.

'Are you right to go?' Erhard whispered, and she managed a smile.

'I like to make my bridegrooms sweat,' she said, and his old face wrinkled into a smile of delight. He looked along the aisle to Nick and she intercepted that look again: *women—we don't understand them but we love them anyway!*

'It's not a real marriage,' Rose whispered, tucking her hand securely into Erhard's. 'This is Nick. Love 'em and leave 'em Nick. I can do this. Let's get this ceremony on the road.'

It wasn't a real marriage. The problem was, though, that it was starting to feel like one. They were standing in church and Nick was making vows that felt…right.

Do you take this woman…?

Rose was beautiful. Not just now, he thought, though beautiful would certainly describe her almost ethereal appearance as she made her vows beside him. The first night in the restaurant she'd taken his breath away. He knew now what lay behind the façade, and it was with almost stunned disbelief that he heard her responses

'I, Rose-Anitra, take you, Nikolai…'

It was mockery. Make believe. *Til death do us part?* No, only until divorce.

But it surely didn't feel like that, and for once he let himself go.

Forget the control. Forget the isolation bit.

He took Rose's hands in his and he held them. Erhard looked on from the sidelines. Hoppy looked on from underneath. And he spoke the words.

'I, Nikolai, take thee, Rose-Anitra… Forsaking all others, keeping myself only unto you, as long as we both shall live.'

It didn't matter, Nick thought almost triumphantly as he kissed her tenderly on the lips in front of the whole congregation. It didn't matter what had been said before or what had been planned for the future

No matter. Things had changed.

He, Nikolai de Montez, was a married man.

* * *

The formalities of the wedding were tedious. Signing, signing and more signing, made longer because Nick decreed there wasn't one document to be signed without checking the wording. Then photography and more photography. And then…

Fun.

A great dance out on the front lawns of the formal palace. At Erhard's suggestion, made by telephone from his convalescence bed, their guest list for the party comprised representatives from every walk of life, from every corner of the country. As many people as were safe to fit squeezed into the grounds, and the festivities were beamed out over the country to where similar celebrations were taking place over and over. The locals looked at their television sets, toasted the bride and groom and allowed themselves to hope. Nick and Rose were dancing their hearts out in each other's arms. This seemed a turning point for this desperately poor principality—it was a new beginning for them and a new beginning for all the country.

Then, as the late hours turned to the small hours, as Rose sagged in exhaustion until all that was holding her up was her husband's arms, the bride and groom were escorted back into the castle and cheered every step as they made their way up the vast marble staircase to the bedchambers beyond.

Nick and Rose. Alone. Even Hoppy had retired long since, sneaking off to find a warm kennel with the kitchen dogs. Tomorrow he'd have Rose to himself, and a dog had to have some beauty sleep.

So for now Nick had Rose all to himself. As they reached the first landing she tripped slightly on her train, and before she knew what he was about he'd swept her up into his arms and carried her the rest of the way. She squeaked in protest, but there was a roar of approval from the crowd below.

'Say goodnight to our friends,' Nick ordered, smiling wickedly down at her and swinging her round so they could both look over the balustrade to the people below. 'Wave.'

She was too dazed to do anything else. She waved.

Nick grinned, swung his bride around and pushed open the first bedroom door.

His.

The door swung closed behind him with a resounding slam.

Another cheer from below, which was just as well, as it disguised the squeak of indignation and the imperious, 'Put me down. Now!'

He put her down. It behoved a man to tread warily when he thought he was married but he wasn't sure where the woman was in the equation. *The earth hadn't moved for her, then?*

'I thought separate bedrooms might be frowned on tonight,' he said.

'By who?'

'By everyone downstairs. You know both our doors are visible from the entrance hall.'

'Then we'll wait until everyone goes away and go to our own rooms.'

'Right,' he said, still cautious. 'You know, you look beautiful.'

'You look pretty gorgeous yourself,' she retorted. 'Gold tassels and a dress sword. Wow.'

'I did scrub up well,' he admitted, and thought fleetingly that if his foster brothers had been here they would have looked at the dress sword and given him a very hard time. But Blake and his brothers had been told not to come—not to a mock wedding; that would have been crazy.

But thinking of his foster family was for later. For now he had to placate his bride—who showed every sign of retreating to her own bedroom.

'I need to go,' she said. 'Even if people see me.'

'It's not a good look—bride bolting for her own room.'

She glowered.

'It was a very nice wedding,' he said, striving to keep his voice normal.

'It was.'

'You don't have to look at me like that,' he complained. 'I'm not about to jump you.'

'You'd better not.'

'Why would you think I'd want to?' he asked and that obviously set her back. The suspicion on her face gave way to confusion.

'You don't want to?'

'Not if you don't.'

'I don't.'

'Not even a little bit?' he asked, and she gasped.

'No. I…'

'I just thought,' he said, seemingly innocent. 'I mean, you've been a widow for a long time, and there are some things… Well, you might be missing sex?'

'That's none of your business.'

'No, but I really enjoy sex,' he said softly, wickedly, thinking well, why not? She was gorgeous. And she was his wife. 'I'd hate to think of my wife as being deprived.'

She gasped again and took two steps backwards.

'Don't you dare.'

'You really don't want…'

'This marriage is a marriage of convenience.'

'So it is. But I think you're beautiful and you think I'm gorgeous.'

'Just your tassels,' she said. Breathlessly.

'You want to see me without my tassels?' he asked, and started unbuttoning his dress coat.

She yelped.

His hand stilled. 'You don't want me to undress?'

'No. No!'

'So this marriage stays unconsummated.'

'Yes,' she said, but suddenly her voice was a little unsure. She was looking at his throat. Why?

She wasn't looking at his face.

'Rose-Anitra.'

'Yes?'

'Have I ever told you that's a beautiful name?'

'Rose.'

'But you're not English,' he said. 'You're a princess of Alp de Montez. You're my wife.'

'You don't have any rights,' she said.

'I know I don't,' he said gently. 'I would never want you to do anything you didn't wish. But if you wished…'

'I don't wish.'

'No.'

He nodded. This room was massive. It was a suite, really, a vast sitting room with an opulent bedchamber attached. He'd been bemused when he'd seen it. 'The master of the castle always uses these rooms,' he'd been told, and he thought he'd better go along with it. But it really was over the top.

There was a vast four-poster bed draped with crimson velvet, edged with gold. Gold tassels a hundred times as large as the ones on his uniform. Gilt furniture, overstuffed. A couple of gilt lions on either side of the blazing fireplace.

'I guess your patients back in Yorkshire wouldn't recognise you now,' he said gently, and she did look at him then and managed a smile.

'No.'

'Your parents-in-law didn't come to the wedding?'

'What do you think?' she said bitterly. 'I asked them, but no. I've betrayed them.'

'How did you betray them?'

'I abandoned Max.'

'Max died,' he said, frowning. 'Two years ago.'

'I didn't have his baby.'

'I see,' he said cautiously, but of course he didn't. 'And the reason you don't want to sleep with me?'

'I'm not in love with you.'

'No, but if you were?' he said, probing something he suddenly sensed was important. She was so lovely. His bride.

Rose's dress was a family heirloom. The palace housekeeper had produced it the same day that the country had installed them in this castle.

'We hid it,' she'd said as she'd presented it to Rose. 'We hid it from your sister because she's not the right one.'

The dress was maybe a hundred years old, exquisite: a clinging bodice and flowing skirt, white silk with gold embroidery, a soft gold underskirt; there was enough color for everyone to decide it was suitable for a widow's remarriage.

'I can't be in love with you,' she said, still breathless. 'Not and be free.'

'I'd never tie you to me.'

Her brow creased into a furrow. 'That sounds almost like a proposal.'

'No, but I was just thinking…' he said, wondering as he said it, what was he thinking? He wasn't sure. It was just… She was so lovely. And she was right here before him, her brow creased with just that little furrow. And he'd made those vows, and suddenly they seemed not so stupid after all. Not so scary.

But she was frightened. She took a step back. 'Nick, we're taking this no further.'

'No.'

'I'd get pregnant,' she said.

Yeah? 'That could happen,' he said cautiously. 'But I read something at the back of a very dark bookstore, somewhere in my deep and murky past, that suggested it might just be possible to prevent it.'

'The only sure contraception is a two-foot-thick brick wall.'

'Have you been talking to my foster mother?' he demanded, but she wasn't smiling.

'I could never have a child.'

He frowned. Up until now he'd felt that this situation right now was light. Fun, even. No, she didn't want to go to bed with him, and he'd never force her. But a bit of light-hearted dalliance after the romance of the day had seemed okay, and if it had led further…

He wouldn't have objected at all. The more he saw of Rose the more desirable she became. Today had been fantastical. They'd been transported into a fairy tale, a make-believe that was for now only. But why not let it run its course? What harm would it have done?

But suddenly the mood had changed. There was bleak heaviness in her voice. *I could never have a child.*

'Is there something wrong?' he asked, aware that he was intruding, but there was such bleakness in her eyes that he felt compelled to.

'There's nothing wrong,' she said.

'But you can't have children?'

'I… No.'

'You and Max tried?'

'No!'

'Oh,' he said. Then, 'You know, this is one thing we haven't thought of.'

'What?'

'The succession.'

'Why would we worry about the succession?'

'If you died then Julianna would inherit.'

'Erhard said we can put changes in place. Permanent changes. This country will never be so dependent on its sovereign again.'

'No,' he said, doubtful.

'Don't you dare tell me it's my duty to have a baby,' she spat, and her voice was suddenly so laced with fury that he stared.

'Hey,' he said, and held his hands up in mock surrender. 'I didn't.'

'You inferred it.'

'I just said it might be fun to learn about how *not* to have babies.' He was trying to make her smile again, but she wouldn't be persuaded.

'Nick, leave it.'

'I'll certainly leave babies,' he said, still rattled. 'I certainly don't want them myself, and if you can't have them then—'

'Then the discussion's ended.'

'Right,' he said, and drew his sword.

'What are you doing with that?' She sounded nervous.

'Hey, Rose, I'm not about to ravish you at sword's point. I thought I might hang it on the hook behind the door,' he said. 'It occurred to me that if I'm promising not to ravish my bride I'd better put down my weapons.'

'All your weapons,' she said.

'There's only my sword.'

'Stop smiling too,' she said, and he paused. Carefully he hung his sword and turned back to her.

'Does my smile do to you what your smile does to me?'

'I… What?'

'You see, there's the problem,' he said. 'There's the crux of the whole mess. Because you're standing there looking absolutely fabulous and you look amused, and then you look angry, and then you look frightened, and you know what? Every single expression you use makes me want to kiss you senseless.'

'Which…which would be a mistake,' she stammered, and her voice wobbled.

'I can see that. But I'm damned if I know what to do about it.'

'I'm sure I can go to my room now.'

'Listen,' he told her. From below came the sound of laughter, many voices settling in for the long haul. 'Did we have to invite so many people?'

'They'll go home soon. I could sneak—'

'Oh, sure. Open the door really, really silently, checking every inch of the way that there's no one in the hall. Crouch on all fours so you're below the level of the balustrade. Crawl slowly along, hoping no one looks up. Oh, and may I remind you that we have guests staying on this floor? Foreign dignitaries from all over. Any one of them could chance along and meet the royal bride crawling bedroom-wards. Wouldn't look good.'

'No,' she agreed, and she smiled, resigned. Damn it, there was that smile again. 'So what do we do?'

'Read,' he said. 'I have a legal brief or six somewhere.'

'Sleep's probably a better idea,' she said. 'I'm exhausted.'

'Me too,' he said, and looked hopefully through the door at the four-poster bed.

'You go to bed,' she told him. 'I'll use the settee.'

The settee was huge. It looked very, very comfortable. Nick looked at it, sighed and knew what his duty was.

'I'm an honourable man,' he said.

'So?'

'So you use the bed and I'll use the settee.'

'But—'

'Don't say it,' he said, and held up his hands in mock surrender. 'I know. Hero is my middle name. Just toss me out four of those feather pillows and two of those duvets, and I'll suffer in silence right here while you wallow in my rightful princely bed.'

She giggled.

He smiled. He'd made her giggle. There was so much about her that he didn't understand. He wanted desperately more and more to kiss her, to get closer to her, to see if, just if, this relationship might go a little further. He'd always been wary of marriage—attachments—but slowly Rose was creeping under his skin in a way he hadn't felt possible.

He'd suggested seduction this night and she'd refused. But instead of feeling wounded he wanted to know why, not for him, but for her. And he liked that he'd made her giggle.

There was something in the baby thing, he thought. He'd get to the bottom of it eventually. But for now he'd brought the laughter back into her eyes and he was quitting while he was ahead.

'Goodnight, my bride,' he said and he took her hands and tugged her forwards and kissed her lightly on the tip of her nose. God only knew how hard it was to leave it at that, but he did. 'Sleep well,' he told her. 'Sleep in your royal bed while your knight errant guards your sleep.'

'My knight errant?'

'I have no idea what that means,' he confessed. 'But it sounds great. It's me. It means I get to go to sleep with my sword.'

When I'd far rather be sleeping with my lady, he added under his breath. He wanted the laughter to stay.

He wanted this lady to smile.

CHAPTER NINE

SHE lay in his too-big bed, dressed in the soft chemise that had been her underskirt during the day. The silk was soft against her body. The feather duvet was so luxurious—so far away from the heavy blankets she'd been used to in Yorkshire—that she felt she was floating.

She was married. *Remarried*, she reminded herself. She'd been married once before, and now she'd made those marriage vows again. Only she had not. She'd lied.

She lay there in Nick's big bed and felt small. And lost. And lonely.

Hoppy was down in the kitchens. She should get up and go find him.

Right—the royal bride padding down through the ancient corridors calling Hoppy, Hoppy, Hoppy…

It'd probably make headline news.

See, that was what she hadn't counted on. This interest. The realisation that this marriage wasn't just between the two of them—it was a marriage for the country. She'd wanted freedom, but what dumb reasoning had had her thinking she could have freedom as a royal bride?

And if she succumbed to Nick's sexiness, the blaze of desire she saw in his eyes every time he looked at her… Where would her freedom be then?

And a child… A baby…

It was closing in on her. Nick was too close, just through the door in the shadows, sleeping. She hoped he was sleeping. The thought that he was awake—as she was—was almost unbearable.

'Nick', she wanted to call, but she didn't.

Think of something else. Think of the good things she could do here. Erhard had been with them tonight, pleased but frail. 'I'm proud of you,' he'd said, and that had been something to hold onto. For some strange reason he almost felt like family. Erhard had known her mother and he'd known her as a child. She remembered him as a solicitous attendant to a sick old man.

He was a link to the past.

Julianna hadn't been here today.

That worried her. Rose should have been accustomed to the loss of her sister by now, but she probably never would be. And the whole set-up worried her—that Julianna thought of her as the enemy. She hadn't thought it through enough.

There were repercussions she hadn't thought of, and she lay there and tried to think of them now, but couldn't, and she felt like…

Like padding out and saying to Nick, 'Move over, I want to share your settee'.

She didn't. How could she?

But sex is fun.

What sort of irresponsible thought was that?

It wasn't a bad thought, she conceded, and she found herself smiling wistfully into the night. She was married. Yes, sex with Nick could be more than fun. But…

The only true contraceptive was a brick wall.

Or a bed and a settee in different rooms.

She sighed again, rolled over and buried her head in her pillows.

A royal bride on her wedding night. Without even her dog to keep her company.

Nick stayed awake for longer than she did. He wasn't a good sleeper—four or five hours usually did him, and tonight even this eluded him. So he was awake when the door opened.

He was drifting, letting his thoughts go where they willed. Which was right through the door to Rose. So at first he thought he dreamed it.

The settee was on the far side of the sitting room, facing the fireplace. The fire had burned down, so there was only a soft glow of embers.

Nick sensed rather than heard the door open; the soft creak of moving hinges was barely audible.

Rose must be up and moving about. But why? Had she passed him? Was she leaving the suite to fetch her dog, or returning to her bedroom?

But then the door closed again, and whoever it was hadn't left. He or she was still in the room. Footsteps went slowly past him, so muted that if he wasn't straining he would never have heard them.

Not Rose. He knew that with a certainty that had nothing to do with logic but everything to do with self-preservation. If it had been Rose going to get her dog he would have heard her go out, and there'd have been no need for her to creep back through the room with stealth. She knew him well enough to accept he wouldn't jump her. Surely.

But if it wasn't Rose, then who?

The settee he was on was ancient, down-filled, a great, squishy, luxurious pile of feathers. No modern springs here to squeak as he moved. So he did move, inch by cautious inch, away from the end of the settee closest to the fire so as he edged around he wasn't in line of sight.

One of Nick's foster brothers, Sam, was in the SAS. From the time Sam had come into Ruby's care as a battered nine-year-old, he'd been intent on joining the armed services. Sam had lived and breathed action comics, James Bond movies, superheroes, and by the time he had been in his mid-teens he was reading how-to manuals that were deadly serious.

There'd never been any money living with Ruby. The boys had been expected to entertain themselves, but they'd never had to think how when Sam had been around. He'd had them organised into Boys' Own adventures every minute he could persuade them to leave off cricket or football.

And Sam's semi-serious instructions came back now: never put your body between an opponent and the light. Never move until you're sure of what you're doing. They'd played tag in the back yard, creeping up on each other, touching and winning by stealth alone.

Boys' fantasies. All of a sudden serious. All of a sudden imperative to remember.

For whoever it was meant no good. Whoever it was, he or she had almost reached the bedroom door. Nick was used to the dim light, and he could see the shadow now. One man, he thought, one man with his back to him. One man, slowly lifting the latch to the bedroom beyond.

The bedroom door opened slowly, slowly.

Hell, he needed a weapon.

The fire-iron. He slid forward, and the cold steel of the massive poker slid soundlessly into his grasp. He moved back, still crouched behind the settee, waiting.

His heart felt as if it had stopped beating. *Sam, where the hell are you?*

Whoever it was had opened the door fully now. There was an almost-full moon. The curtains in the sitting room were drawn but Rose must have opened hers, letting the moonlight flood her as she slept. As the bedroom door opened wide, Nick had a clear, full view of the man's silhouette. Long and lean and all in black. One hand on the door handle.

The other… The other holding a gun.

How he moved, he didn't remember afterwards. The man's arm was raising. He was moving inside the bedroom, intent, concentrating fiercely on his target. His hand came up further…

And Nick's poker smashed down with all the force he could muster.

He must have made a sound, slight but a sound for all that, for the man jerked to one side so that the poker didn't smash down on his head but hit him hard, sickeningly, where neck met shoulder, then slid down, still with force, smashing into his gun-arm, causing the gun to drop and skid and spin across the room.

And Nick had him, hauling him round, bringing his knee up, fighting foul as he'd learned to fight with six brothers. Ruby had hated their fighting, but they'd all been brought up tough and they knew the ways of the world. They'd practised constantly. Every single one of Ruby's boys had learned the hard way that you could never depend on others to defend you.

But the man whirled and smashed back. Nick was too close to raise the poker again. He punched with all the power he had.

'Rose!' Nick roared as the man staggered against the wall, and he powered in again. 'Get the gun.'

'Wha…?' Wakened from deep sleep, it took Rose all of two seconds to snap to wakefulness. 'The gun?' she said blankly.

'Under the bed, your side!' Nick yelled, and hit the guy again. If this guy knew any martial arts, Nick was in big trouble. Nick was a lawyer. Yeah, he'd learned to fight, but he hadn't fought for years. But he wasn't giving the guy room to do anything, punching him against the wall, hitting him, hitting him until the guy lashed out again…

'Move one muscle and I'll shoot.' Rose's voice rang out clearly over the moonlit room. The night-light snapped on.

She must have been brought up in the same school as him, Nick thought approvingly, for she'd flicked the bed-lamp on and moved away up to the back of the bed so *she* could see but was in the shadows.

All the same, he could see enough to know she had the gun.

He moved back, which was a mistake. The guy lurched forward and his hand suddenly glinted in the light.

A knife…

The gun fired, a heavy, dull pop into the stillness. And everyone froze. For a moment.

The black figure cursed, grabbed his shoulder and lurched backwards. The knife, a wicked-looking stiletto, clattered onto the bedroom floor and slid harmlessly away.

'I'll shoot again,' Rose said in a voice devoid of all inflection. 'I'd advise you to keep very still indeed.'

The guy did. So did Nick. This seemed dream-like. Like a game with his brothers. But it was no dream. He was wide awake now and he felt sick.

Hell, she'd shot the man…

'Back against the wall,' Rose said, still in that cold, dead tone, and she jumped lightly from the bed and flicked the overhead light on. Nick grabbed the huge gold tassel of the bell-pull and pulled for all he was worth.

The bell pealed out so loudly that you could have heard it in the middle of next week. Not a nice, discreet, 'hear it only in the butlers pantry' bell. If the old Prince had wanted something he'd wanted the whole castle to know about it. The man made an involuntary lurch towards the door.

'Still,' she snapped. 'I will shoot.'

'Rose…'

'Get right away from him,' Rose said.

He couldn't believe it. She was standing in her chemise, barefoot, her hair tousled from sleep, her face deathly pale. She was holding the gun in both hands and she was aiming it straight at the intruder.

The intruder had frozen. And why wouldn't he? The man was young, thickset, dressed all in black with a balaclava covering his face. He was holding his arm, and blood was dripping slowly onto the polished floor.

And then there were people in the doorway. An elderly liveried manservant. A couple of dignitaries who were staying in the castle, in their nightwear. And behind them, blessedly, one of the castle security-guards. The man edged through the crowded doorway and stopped dead in astonishment.

'He came to kill us,' Nick said.

Rose hadn't moved. She was still pointing the gun directly at the man before her. 'Can I put it down?' she whispered.

'Let's get back-up first,' Nick said, and looked expectantly at the security guard, and the guard took a shocked look at Rose and moved into action. He spoke urgently into his radio.

And suddenly things were out of their hands.

The next hour passed in a blur. The security guards took their intruder down to one of the main sitting-rooms, where those who had no direct cause to be present could be closed out.

Nick called Erhard. The old man was a guest this night in the castle. Nick didn't want to disturb him, but faced with what might have happened, faced with the evil he'd seen tonight, he needed to be sure who he could trust.

Erhard arrived in bathrobe and carpet slippers, looking pale, old and shaken to the core, but still retaining the aura of dignity that he'd carried from the first.

'I'm so sorry,' he told Rose, his voice trembling. 'I would never have asked you if…'

'It's alright,' Rose said, but she wasn't moving from where she was. Which was tight against Nick. From the moment Nick had lifted the pistol out of her hands, she'd started trembling and the trembling hadn't stopped. Nick had wanted her to be put to bed, for the doctors here to give her something to help her sleep, but she'd reacted with anger, and momentarily the trembling had stopped.

'Someone tried to shoot me, so I'm supposed to take a sleeping tablet and go calmly to sleep without getting it sorted? You must be out of your collective minds.' Then as Nick had held her she'd subsided against him and let him do the supporting. 'I have a husband,' she said with dignity. 'When he goes to bed, I go to bed, and not before.'

She'd held to that line, as more onlookers had spilled from the surrounding bedrooms, as every member of the castle staff had seemed to find some excuse to see for themselves what was happening.

Little was happening. The security guards had held their prisoner until Erhard had arrived.

'These men can be trusted,' Erhard told Nick, nodding to each of the four security-guards. 'I know each of them. But I don't understand how—'

'There was a disturbance on the far side of the castle grounds,' one of the guards told Erhard, sounding appalled and apologetic at the same time. 'The fence was slashed and a group of youths tried to break in. They were young and drunk and foolish, but we all attended.' He hesitated. 'There's only been the old Prince here for so long,' he said. 'There's been no interest in the castle. My officers have been lax.'

'There's been little need for security in the past,' Erhard said gravely. 'But there is now. What chance these youths were paid to make a distraction?'

'I'll find out,' the senior guard said grimly. He looked at the man they were holding. Rose's bullet had clipped his skin, a surface wound. One of the guards had roughly bandaged it to stop it bleeding. The man stood now between two guards, grim-faced, silent. 'As we'll find out who this is.'

'And who's paying him,' Erhard said heavily. 'Can you triple your numbers here tonight, using trusted people only? I want people outside and in the corridors.' Then he turned to Rose. 'I'm so sorry,' he said again. 'We weren't prepared. You'll be safe now.'

'I had Nick,' she said.

'Yes.' The old man's eyes met Nick's. 'Without you…'

'It was Rose who did the shooting.'

'Thank you both,' he said grimly. 'My two…' He hesitated, and appeared to think better of what he'd been about to say. 'We'll keep you safe,' he said roughly, and turned and walked away, signalling the guards and their prisoner to follow.

They were left alone.

'I think we should go fetch Hoppy,' Nick said, and as they walked out of the sitting-room door they had to walk past two burly security guards.

Two more appeared from nowhere and escorted them to the kitchens.

They retrieved Hoppy. Their guards followed at a respectable distance as they made their way upstairs again.

'Not your room,' Rose said urgently, hugging Hoppy close, and Nick nodded.

'Okay, sweetheart,' he said. There'd still be blood on the floor. He could understand. 'But I'll walk you to your door.'

'Not…' She took a deep, shuddering breath. 'I meant *both* of us not to your bedroom. I thought maybe you'd come to mine?'

The security guards behind them had paused. They stayed, impassive. Maybe they didn't follow English, Nick thought hopefully.

'Of course,' he said. It was totally understandable that she didn't want to stay in the bedroom by herself, he thought. So why his heart should lurch…

'Thank you,' she said simply, and they didn't say another word until they were in her suite with the door locked behind them. Securely, with a key, and the key stayed on the inside of the door, with a bolt besides.

Rose placed Hoppy on the floor. Hoppy looked up at his mistress, and gave a sleepy wag of his tail; it was four in the morning, after all, and a dog had need of beauty sleep. He hopped through to the big bed in the next room, leaped lightly up onto the pillows and proceeded to go back to sleep.

'Great watchdog,' Nick said, and smiled.

'I think we're safe tonight,' she said.

'Yes.'

'It'll have been Jacques.'

'Probably,' he said.

'And Julianna.' She was still deathly pale. Dressed only in her chemise, she was shivering. It was warm enough, and the fire made it more so, but still she shook. 'Julianna's my sister,' she said, distressed. 'I never dreamed…' She shuddered. 'She must hate me. I never thought. Back home this seemed so simple, but how did we ever think we could do it, take over a throne just like that? You know, somehow, because Julianna was planning to do it herself, it seemed possible. Feasible, even. Marry you. Have the great adventure. Save a country. It's the stuff of storybooks where there are happy endings and everything's resolved by…I don't know kissing a frog.'

She hiccupped on a sob and he reached for her and tugged her against him, holding her, simply holding her as she sobbed and sobbed. The front of his shirt grew wet from her weeping, but still she wept, great, shuddering sobs that wracked her whole body.

He held her for as long as it took. But finally she cried herself out. He felt her body go limp. He was half-supporting her. She felt so… So…

So much his wife.

That was what it felt like. It felt like he had all the time in the world. It felt that indeed this was his wedding night, or more, that this was his wedding moment. He'd sworn never to fall in love, but he had, he had. If she'd been killed tonight…

He kissed her gently, wonderingly, on the top of her head, and maybe he shuddered himself for she drew back a little and looked up at him in the firelight.

'I'm s-sorry,' she said, hiccupping slightly as she tried to find her voice. 'I don't cry.'

'I can see that about you.'

'No, really,' she said, and somehow she made her voice firm. 'I don't. I don't know what I'm about tonight.'

'You shot a man,' he said gently. 'How you did that…' He felt his gut clench at the thought of what she'd done. 'How the hell did you do it?' he asked, thinking it through. 'To wake up and get the gun and actually fire the thing?'

'I'm a vet,' she said simply.

'I'm not sure that that explains it fully.' He tugged her close again, not because he needed to—oh, fine, yes, he needed to—but not for comfort. Just because this was Rose.

His wife!

'I deal with big animals,' she said.

'And?'

'And I had to learn to deal with firearms. The first time I ever needed to… Well, there was an injured bull. There was no way I could get near it, but I couldn't leave it. The farmer handed me his gun and expected me to use it.'

'He handed *you* the gun?' What sort of wimp had this guy been?

'Farmers get attached to their animals. It's hard to put them down.'

'So you did.'

'Not that time,' she said. 'I couldn't. I… Well, the farmer had to do it, and it took him two shots and he cried. I went home that night and said I couldn't do it, and my father-in-law said he'd take the practice back over for a week while I did a firearms course.'

'He what?' Hell. 'Where was Max in all this?'

'Ill. He was only well for a short time.'

'So you had to do the shooting?'

'Not often.' But he could hear it in her voice—too often.

'Did you want to do big-animal stuff?'

'I'd started vet school wanting to look after dogs,' she said, and sniffed. 'And cats and canaries and kids' tortoises. Cases where sheer strength isn't an issue when an animal's in pain.' She was hugged against him as naturally as if she belonged there. 'But the family needed me.'

'Max's family. And now your family's trying to kill you,' he said. 'You've had a rum deal.'

'No.' She hugged him a bit closer while she thought about it. Which was fine with him. More than fine. 'I asked for this,' she said at last. 'But it's been a shock…that Julianna would…' She hesitated. 'Maybe she didn't know.'

'Maybe she didn't. Maybe it wasn't even Jacques.'

'Do you think whoever it was really meant to kill us?'

'Yes.' There was no point in lying to her. The man behind the gun hadn't hesitated, he had aimed at the figure in the bed with one thought in mind. He'd have been expecting there to be two in the bed. Maybe the far side of the bed had been in shadow, but he'd had six bullets in the chamber. He'd come to kill. He'd even brought a knife as a back-up, to finish the job if he had to.

Rose knew it as well as he did. He felt her shudder and held her tighter.

'Julianna's my sister,' she whispered bleakly. 'My family. There's no one else.'

He couldn't bear it. 'There is someone else,' he said, pulling her hard against him so strongly that he could feel her heartbeat against his. 'You have a husband. As of today. It's time someone took care of you. It's time.'

'You're only here for four weeks or so.'

'I'll stay for as long as you need me.'

'I don't… I don't think…'

'You don't need to think. Leave thinking for the morning, sweetheart,' he told her. 'You're done.'

'I am.' She hesitated. 'Hoppy's asleep on the bed.'

'So he is. You want me to shift him to the settee?'

'I… No. It seems a shame to shift him.'

Right. Rose's suite was the same as his. A living room with fire. Bedroom through the farther door. From where he stood her bed looked vast. Far too big for one. There was plenty of room for Rose to sleep and not disturb the dog. But…

'Nick?'

'Mmm?'

'You wouldn't like to share the settee with me?'

There was a moment's pause while he thought about it. Her heartbeat was synchronised with his, he thought, and it felt fine. It felt right.

Share the settee. To sleep. But the way he was thinking of her… 'If we did that,' he said cautiously, 'we might just…'

'Yes,' she said, and it was an answer to a question he hadn't asked.

'Yes?'

'Yes,' she said again, and she smiled.

He put her at arm's length, searching her face in the moonlight. Astounded. 'Rose, are you sure?'

'Yes.'

'But you were so sure we shouldn't.'

'Yes, but things have changed,' she whispered. 'For tonight, it's not the same. I don't want to be an adventurer for tonight. What I'd really like is to be a wife.'

'You are my wife,' he said.

'Yes.'

'And you're sure?'

'Yes.' And she smiled again.

He kissed her then, softly, sweetly. Wonderously. She melted into his kiss, and her arms wound round his neck and held.

'Yes,' she said again. 'Nick, I need you. Please, I need you in my bed. You're my husband, Nick, and I want to be your wife.'

And then, suddenly, before any more of these stupid scruples could get in the way, she tugged her chemise over her head. Underneath she was wearing scant lacy knickers. Nothing more. With her eyes not leaving his face, she slipped them down and let them fall, stepping out of them and taking a step back.

Standing before him in the firelight. Gloriously naked.

His wife.

Her auburn curls, loose and floating round her shoulders, almost seemed to be dancing in the firelight. Her eyes were too big in her too-pale face. Yet she smiled, tremulously, as if she wasn't sure what she was offering was wanted.

How could she doubt that?

He caught her hands and held her out from him, glorying in her nakedness. Glorying in the fact that this could be happening. That such a woman could want him.

That such a woman could be his wife.

The words he'd spoken this afternoon came back to him, and they seemed so right. How could he ever have thought he'd never marry? He hadn't understood until tonight what it was. Marriage. The joining of man and woman, making one.

But he needed to be sure. He wouldn't take this woman unless she understood…

'Rose, there's the contraceptive thing.'

'There's condoms in my toiletries bag,' she told him, and he almost gasped.

'But you said…'

'I know what I said,' she told him. 'But I was coming here to be married to the world's sexiest man, and a girl would have to be crazy not to plan for all eventualities.'

The world's sexiest man…

He needed to put that aside. 'But if there's a baby?'

'There won't be.'

'Rose…'

'Okay, there might be,' she said. 'Slight chance. I'm risking it.'

'Earlier tonight you wouldn't.'

'Earlier tonight I was ten years younger than I am now. Nick, I need you. Are you saying no?'

'Not just for sex, Rose.' He shook his head, confused, but at some deep level understanding that he was in uncharted territory. This was important. A voice in the back of his head was hammering with dogged insistence, *get this right.*

He'd never felt like this about a woman, and he wouldn't mess with it for want of patience, or for want of restraint, no matter how much that restraint might cost. He wouldn't risk her waking in the morning and reacting with horror at what they'd done. 'This needs to be an act of love,' he said, and as he said it he knew that it was right. Something was changing inside him. Something he hadn't been aware could be changed.

She was smiling in the firelight, standing on tiptoes so she could kiss him. His hands dropped to her waist, and the feel of her silk-smooth skin…

If she was to move away she had to do it now, he thought, and his thoughts were getting a little blurred. He was offering her the chance to change her mind, but a man was only human. If she said no now…

She did no such thing.

She lifted one of his hands from her waist, lifting it high so the back of his hand was against her cheek. So she could feel the roughness of his skin against her. Then she moved his hand slowly down, gently guiding it so the palm of his hand was cupping her breast.

It seemed she had no doubts. For this night, she was his wife. For this night, their vows would hold.

The terrors of the night, overwhelming, appalling, out of their world, were slipping away now as if they'd been a bad dream. This was the reality, and only this. She put her hands up and touched his face gently, tenderly, never letting her eyes move from his.

'Nick.'

He bent and he kissed her.

And in that instant, her world readjusted. The awful tilting somehow righted itself. For this wondrous moment, the horrors of the night and the bleakness of the past few years made way for…

For Nick. For loving. For wonder. Nick's mouth was on hers, and he tasted wonderful. His hands were on her waist, tugging her against him. His hands were a man's hands, big, strong, but caressing with a tenderness that made her want to weep. But the time for weeping was past. She was tracing the contours of his cheeks with her fingers, feeling the roughness of the beginning of stubble, glorying in his sheer masculinity. It had been too long since she'd held a man. Any man. She'd loved Max, but for years he'd been ill, and her touch had needed to be tender. She'd been the one doing the giving.

Not here. Not now. She could feel the strength in Nick, the unleashed power, and she wanted it, oh, she wanted it. But she'd never guessed until this moment how much.

He was deepening the kiss, and she gloried in it. Her lips parted, and her tongue did its own exploring. Her breasts were pressed hard against him, against the soft linen of his shirt, feeling the strength of his chest. Feeling...

All she was doing was feeling. All she wanted to do was to feel. He'd kept his trousers and his shirt on during all the troubles of this night, but she wanted them gone now. But to ask him to remove them—to remove them herself—was to break the moment. And how could she?

It was Nick who paused. It was Nick who moved back, just a little, holding her at arm's length so he could look into her eyes. His eyes were dark in the firelight, almost black, and when he spoke his voice was deep and husky with desire.

'This is love-making,' he said softly. 'Rose, what we're doing, it's because of love. I should say...'

She knew what he wanted to say. This was a marriage of convenience. A marriage for a month. He wanted no commitment, and he was an honourable man.

Too honourable. When she wanted this so much.

'We can be in love only for tonight,' she whispered, knowing it was what he wanted to hear. It was what she wanted herself—wasn't it? But she no longer knew and she no longer cared. Tomorrow was for tomorrow. 'For now, yes, I'm loving you. I just want you to love me. Please, Nick. Now.'

The 'now' didn't quite work. For she couldn't quite form the word before her lips were claimed again. Her mouth was being plundered by his, his hands were tugging her close, pulling her up against him, almost lifting her in a long, triumphant, loving kiss where the night dissolved around them and doubts were swept away, and there was only Nick in her world. And there was room for nothing else.

She closed her eyes, her whole body responding with sensual pleasure as he deepened the kiss. She was holding his face in her hands, aching for him to be closer, closer. His hands were in the small of her back, pressing her against him, sending shivers of ecstasy though her whole body. Nick… Her man.

Her hands slipped under the fine fabric of his shirt, tugging him against her, moulding to him, letting him take her weight as she gloried in the strength of him. For Rose, who'd had to be strong for so long, to let go now, to let this man take her…

This was some romantic fantasy that was suddenly, gloriously real. This was happening in truth and not in dreams. She'd married this man today. This was her husband. She had every right to demand that he take her, as he could demand that she surrender. Glorious surrender. Only it worked both ways, this surrender. She was plundering him as he was plundering her. As he was surrendering to her. He groaned softly into the night and she thought, yes, he was out of control and so was she, and this was their right.

His mouth was moving now. Still he held her against him so her feet were barely on the floor, but he had total control. He kissed her as she ached to be kissed. Her neck, her lips, her eyelids. She arched her neck and let him do as he willed, her body heating as she'd never known it could heat. Her whole world centred around the pattern he was making with his tongue.

He was lowering her now, to the rug before the fire, following her down, his hands, his mouth still conjuring their magic. But he was still in his clothes. She needed him closer. She wanted his skin against hers. She wanted his body, and this man was her husband. She had the right.

She pulled back, just a little. The flickering firelight was lighting his face, shadows and contours, illuminating the strength of his bone structure, showing the passion deep in his eyes. A passion that she was sure was matched in her own.

He watched her, intent, tracking every expression as her fingers unfastened the buttons of his shirt. She was lying full-length against him, side by side, and she could feel his breathing deepening as she made her way downward. Button by button. Slow but sure. There was no rush. She had all the time in the world, and this was her man.

His shirt was gone now, and she couldn't think how. She didn't need to know how. She shifted downward a little and pushed him back, just slightly, so he rolled onto his back and she could lie her cheek on his chest. His fingers caressed her hair as she kissed his chest. She found his nipples, one after the other, tasted them in turn, teased them with her tongue and felt him groan again. He was at her mercy. Her man. Hers.

She pulled herself over him so her body lay full-length on his. She tugged his arms up, holding them, then lowering her mouth so she could kiss him as he needed to be kissed. Then her own arms were captured and he pulled her upward, lifting her higher. She lay motionless, gasping her pleasure as his tongue found her breasts. Slowly. Slowly. He explored each breast and kissed them in turn, taking her sensory aware-ness to a new plane, a place she'd never known was there...

He rolled her sideways then, so they were side by side again. Her lips cried out a protest, but this time it was needful. His mouth claimed hers again, but she felt his fingers fumble for the catch of his pants. Yes. Her fingers moved to help him and his kiss stopped, and he gave a low chuckle of pure, sensory pleasure.

'I can undress myself, Madam Wife.'

'Not fast enough—my husband,' she murmured, and she chuckled and tugged the zip down in one triumphant tug. Away. He'd have to do the rest himself, for as his trousers disappeared her hands stayed where they were.

She was going nowhere. This was what she wanted most in the entire world. There was nothing except this place, this time, this man. She'd made her vows and this was her right.

How could she have wanted this to be a marriage on paper only? How could she have denied herself this joy? Yes, this was for now. Nick had no want of an everyday wife, and she wanted her freedom. Or she *thought* she wanted her freedom. But that was for tomorrow and to deny herself this pleasure, this wonder, this sensation that she was where she most wanted to be in the world, that she had at last found her home…

'Where did you say this condom was?' he growled, and she came as near as a hair's width of saying 'no, no need', for to lose him now, to have him move away… But somehow sense prevailed; somehow she managed to whisper directions; somehow she made herself release him and wait and hold her breath in case the magic was lost…

But then he was back, sinking down onto the wonderful thick fireside-rug, smiling down at her in the moonlight and making love to her with his eyes.

'And now,' he whispered softly, in a slow, sensual whisper that made her body tingle with aching need. 'And now…'

He was above her, lowering himself with tantalising slowness. Skin against skin, not all at once but inch by glorious inch, until they lay full-length naked against each other.

Oh, the wonder of him. He was kissing her neck, her breasts, a rain of kisses, while his wonderful hands caressed her body, her navel, her belly and beyond.

He was so beautiful. He was…Nick.

The fire crackled, spitting out a tiny shower of sparks like an exclamation mark into the night. She could hear the fire, hear Nick's breathing, and she'd never felt so alive as she did at this moment.

'Nick,' she whispered.

'My love?'

'I want you.'

'Not half as much as I want you,' he whispered, and he shifted, pushing himself upward, holding her firm within the strong bounds of his thighs. She gasped with pleasure, with aching need, arched upward, aching to be closer, closer, closer.

Nick.

He was too slow. She held his hips and tugged

him forwards but he leaned forward and kissed her, slowly, languorously, a foretaste of what was to come.

'My Rose,' he whispered. 'My wife.'

'I need you.' Her thighs were aching with need, her body was creating a flame all of its own, but still he resisted. He smiled at her, his smile a caress, and then he kissed her. He moved dreamily downward, tasting her, loving her, moving from lips to neck to belly and beyond, until she was ready to cry with frustration and pleasure and want, and aching, throbbing need.

This was no one-sided love match, she thought as her need took over. This was her man. Her husband. The last dreary years—the fear of Max's illness, a husband who had no strength to take her, a desolate widowhood—they had been far too long to wait a moment longer to take what she most wanted in the whole world.

Nick…

He was rising again, thinking where next his mouth should explore, but she was no longer interested in his mouth. With a fierceness that surprised him her hands moved to have, to hold, to centre him exactly where he needed to be centred.

'My love,' she whispered, and he was there. He was where she most needed him to be.

And he came down, deep, deep inside her,

strong and gentle, plundering yet loving. She arched, wanting him deeper, deeper. She moved with him, moving sensuously on the fireside rug as he needed her to move, letting him take her where he wanted, but assuaging her own need, taking her to where she was meant to be.

She loved him. For this moment she loved him, and how could she not? She was wedded to this man, and that he could be her husband left her wide-eyed with wonder. Her husband. Her mate.

But then she stopped thinking as her body reacted in the most primeval of ways. This was meant to happen—a man taking a woman unto him and becoming one. That was how she felt, as if she was dissolving and becoming part of him, losing a part of herself and gaining him in turn. The warmth, the dark and the firelight, the terrors of the immediate past and the bleakness of the last few years, none of them could impinge on what was happening here—this wondrous fulfilment of passion that had her body taking its need, and causing the night around them to merge into a mist of heat and firelight and white-hot love.

It went on and on, blissfully, achingly, magically, and the moment the sensation eased another started to build. Over and over.

And when it finished, when finally they lay back exhausted, still she held him. Her Nick. Who knew what tomorrow held? But for tonight she was where she was meant to be. She was in her husband's arms.

They rolled until they were side by side. The fire was warm in the small of her back. Somehow she found the energy to pull away, just far enough so she could kiss him tenderly on the mouth. So she could smile at him in the firelight and watch him smile back. She loved his smile. She loved the way his eyes crinkled at the corners. She loved *Nick*.

'Thank you,' she whispered.

'Thanks?' Surprise was mixed with the remnants of spent passion. 'You're thanking me? Rose, do you have any idea how beautiful you are? You're the most desirable woman.' He groaned. 'And how do you think I can walk away after that?'

Her thoughts clouded a little. Just a little, as reality returned.

But tomorrow was for tomorrow. She refused to let it cloud right now.

'We should go to sleep,' she whispered.

'Hoppy has the bed.'

'So he has.'

'Are you warm?' he asked, and she chuckled.

'You're really asking that?'

'I guess I'm not,' he said, and kissed her again. 'Do you really want to go to sleep?'

'I guess.'

'You *guess*?'

'Maybe not.'

'Good,' he said, and tugged her to him again. 'Good, my love. Hoppy has the bed and he needs his beauty sleep. But you don't need beauty sleep, for how could you be any more beautiful than you are right now? So, if you don't need beauty sleep, have you any more suggestions as to how we can fill the time?'

'I'm guessing here,' she said, smiling at him. 'Maybe twenty questions?'

'There is that,' he said with mock seriousness. 'Or "I spy".'

'Maybe we could find that pack of cards.'

'I have another suggestion,' he said, and lifted himself up so his eyes were gleaming down at her in the firelight. 'It's a really good suggestion.'

'What…what is it?'

'That's for me to know and you to find out,' he whispered. 'Just lie back my love, think of England and let me show you.'

CHAPTER TEN

MORNING came too soon.

Or maybe it wasn't morning. Rose stirred where she lay. She was still before the fire, which was now a pile of glowing embers in the grate. At some stage of the night Nick had thrown on another log, and fetched pillows and a vast down-filled duvet, so as the fire had died they'd stayed warm. She was still cradled against his body, the small of her back pressed gently into the curve of his chest. As if she belonged there.

There was a soft knock on the door. Maybe that was what had woken her. She lifted Nick's wrist a little so she could see his watch—and she yelped.

But, instead of releasing her, Nick's arms held her tighter. He nuzzled her ear and she felt rather than heard his low chuckle.

'Going somewhere, wife?'

'The door…Nick, it's two in the afternoon.'

'Golly,' he said, and hugged her still tighter, and

kissed the nape of her neck. She giggled and rolled sideways, sighed and reluctantly sat up. The sun was entering through the chinks in the drapes. Hoppy was sitting on the settee looking down at them with lop-sided concern.

The knock sounded again, gently insistent. The world wanted to come in. Whoever it was wasn't going away.

Nick reached for his trousers. 'Just roll away while I open the door,' he told her.

'Roll where?'

'Somewhere.' He smiled down at her. 'You want to be found naked on the sitting-room floor?'

'Hmm.' She smiled back up at him. Last night someone had tried to kill her, yet right now she felt light and free and deliriously happy.

'Roll,' he told her, and he leaned over, bundled the duvet round her and pushed.

She chuckled, and rolled behind the settee, and then wiggled a bit so she was obediently out of sight. Nick walked to the door, bare-chested. Rose peeked out from behind the settee—and there were her panties right where she'd stepped out of them the night before. 'Nick, wait…'

Too late. 'Yes?' Nick said, and opened the door.

It was a maid, one of the normally somber, uni-formed staff who kept the wheels of domesticity turning. At the sight of Nick, naked from the waist up, she gasped.

'Can we help you?' Nick said politely.

'If you please, sir,' she said, but she ran out of words. She was gazing at his chest, then looking past him. Her mouth sagged open.

'Yes?' he said encouragingly, and she gasped again.

'I…Monsieur Erhard has asked me to tell you…'

'Mmm?'

She swallowed and made an Herculean effort to get things straight. 'He wants to see you. He says… He says he's sorry, but it's urgent. We told him you hadn't had breakfast, so he's asked us to serve croissants and juice in the conservatory.'

'I think we might have breakfast in our room,' Nick said.

The girl had spotted the panties now. Her lips were pressed together. Hard. In disapproval?

'I… No,' she said, and pressed her lips closed again.

'No?'

'Monsieur Erhard says you have company,' she said. Desperately. Clamping her lips tight together again.

'Company?'

'Monsieur Erhard himself. And the Princess Julianna, the Princess Rose-Anitra's sister. And a lady I don't know. She says she knows you and her name is Ruby.'

'Ruby,' Nick said blankly.

'If you please, sir, they're all in the conservatory, and Monsieur Erhard says maybe you could be down in half an hour, but if there was anything you needed before then… um… anything at all…'

'I believe we have everything we need,' Nick said, attempting to sound severe, and the girl's tight-lipped expression finally cracked.

'Yes, sir,' she said, and she smiled. And then she giggled. 'Yes, sir, I see that you do.'

'You realise discipline in this castle is shot to pieces?'

'Yes,' said Rose, chuckling more than the girl had chuckled, and hugging Hoppy as she rolled back out from behind the settee. 'I believe they're my knickers you're standing on, sir.'

He bent and picked them up. They were pink and white and lacy, with butterflies embroidered on them.

'My God,' he said with reverence. 'And I stood on them. Why didn't I notice these last night? Were these special for your wedding?'

'Of course,' she said, and then she giggled again. 'Nope. I tell a lie. I wear knickers like this all the time.'

'You're kidding me.' He held them to the light as one might hold up a piece of priceless art. 'You wear these? As a country vet?'

'I wear brown, grungy overalls and mud, and I smell like cattle,' she said. 'I have to be a girl some time.'

'It's a tragedy,' he said, awed. 'All that time they've been under brown overalls?'

'Um…' She choked back another giggle, then thought about what the girl had said and suddenly it was easy to stop laughing. 'She said Julianna was here.'

'And Ruby,' Nick said, in a tone of deep foreboding.

'Ruby?'

'If it's the Ruby I think it is, it's my foster mother.'

'Your foster mother.' She gathered her duvet round her and rose awkwardly to her feet. 'I didn't…' She frowned. 'You didn't ask her to the wedding?'

'I sort of did. I told her she was welcome but it was a political move, business only, and there was no reason for her to come. Did you ask your in-laws?' he retaliated.

'As a matter of fact I did,' she said. 'Not only did they know why I was coming here, I told them the date of the wedding, and I told them they'd be welcome. Gladys slammed the phone down on me. So why does Ruby's arrival make you sound scared?'

'Because.'

She grinned. 'You sound about ten years old. Because *why*?'

'Because she'll care.'

'I see,' she said cautiously. 'And this would be a disaster?'

'She'll hate that it's not a real marriage,' he said. 'She'll hate that it's a fraud.'

It was like a slap. Rose stilled.

'A fraud,' she whispered. 'I… Oh, yes. Sorry.'

'She's always wanted her boys to marry,' he said, not seeing her dismay as he concentrated on the possible consequences of Ruby's arrival. 'She married for love, and it's her ambition to see us fall in love just like her. She'd never understand why we did this. But Ruby knows I go my own road. Why she's here now…'

'And Julianna,' Rose whispered, pushing aside Nick's troubles in the face of her own. 'Why would she be here? She was invited to the wedding, but she didn't come either. I haven't seen her since that awful night.'

'And they're all waiting for us in the conservatory,' Nick said morosely. 'You think we ought to knot sheets and escape through the window?'

'It's hardly dangerous,' she said.

'If Ruby's mad at me it might be.'

'If Ruby's mad at you then you deserve something dire.'

'Hey, you're on my side.'

'Says who? Can I have my panties, please?'

'Are you going to put them on?'

'I think bluebirds today,' she said with dignity. 'Can I remind you—sir—that this is my bedroom, and all my clothes are here, and everything you own is in your bedroom down the hall? Therefore you should leave.'

'Right,' he said. Dazed. 'Bluebirds.' He almost visibly swallowed. 'But Rose?'

'Yes?'

'I'll wait for you at the head of the stairs,' he told her. 'I think we should go down together.'

'There's safety in numbers?'

'I hope there is,' he said.

Nick returned to his bedroom. The domestic staff had been before him. All evidence of the night's intrusion had disappeared. He showered and dressed as fast as he could, then returned to the head of the stairs.

Rose was already waiting for him. 'How the…?'

'You obviously take longer putting on your make-up than I do,' she told him, and smirked and started down the stairs.

She was wearing ancient jeans, an oversized sweatshirt and shabby sneakers. She'd tugged her hair back into a simple ponytail. Her face was scrubbed clean of all make-up. Anyone further from the elegant bride of yesterday he couldn't imagine.

But somewhere under those jeans were blue-birds. He stood at the top of the stairs and forgot to move, so she had to stop at the first landing and turn to him, exasperated.

'Coming?'

'Sure,' he said uncertainly, and she grinned.

'I couldn't find the bluebirds. It's bumblebees.'

He nearly tripped and fell all the way to the bottom. Somehow he kept his feet and managed to follow her through the maze of corridors to the conservatory. *Bumblebees.* They passed three of the domestic staff on their way, and each had a smile as wide as a house plastered on their faces.

This wasn't a house shocked to the core by news of an assassination attempt, he thought. Their movements since the intrusion had obviously been noted and were giving pleasure. Maybe news of the butterflies was winging its way round the castle right now.

But not the bumblebees. He was feeling decidedly proprietary about those bumblebees.

His mind was having trouble focusing on anything it should be focusing on, and it was almost a relief when they reached the conservatory and Rose pushed open the door. This was an orangery, a conservatory planned in the days when oranges had been an inconceivable luxury in a climate too cold for them. There were orange trees in beautifully ordered lines under the magnificent glass-roof. A truly royal tiled floor—a coat of arms in tiles—was magnificent enough to take the breath away.

But Nick scarcely saw it. There was a table in the bow window at the end of the long, glass-panelled conservatory. There were three people sitting at it.

Erhard. Julianna.

Ruby.

Uh-oh.

Maybe he shouldn't have told her, he thought nervously. But she'd have found out anyway. Ruby was a diminutive white-haired lady. She was dressed in her customary pastel twin-set, tweed skirt and sensible shoes. A string of pearls her foster sons had given her for her sixtieth birthday showed she'd considered this day worth dressing up for, but there was little of the celebration about her small person now. She looked very, very hostile.

She rose, and Nick had the same urge to run that he'd had when he'd been ten years old and she'd discovered him 'making lollies'—rolling dollops of butter in brown sugar and eating them with delicious abandonment. Half a pound of butter had disappeared before she'd found him.

'Nikolai Jean Louis de Montez,' she said now, in exactly the same voice as she'd used then. 'What do you think you're doing?'

He had an almost irresistible urge to hold Rose in front of him like a shield. Only the knowledge that Rose was staring at Julianna like she was seeing a ghost stopped him.

'I did say I'd fly you over if you wanted to come,' he said weakly, and Ruby stalked towards him with such determined anger that for an awful moment he was afraid she'd box his ears.

When had she ever, though? Even after 'the butter incident' she'd simply made him walk the two miles to the nearest dairy to buy some more, and then go without butter on his toast for a week.

But she was angry. Boy, was she angry.

'You told me,' she said icily, 'that you were marrying a European princess in name only so she could claim the throne. You said it wasn't a real marriage. A contract only, if I'm not mistaken. Two signatures on a piece of paper. Why would I want to come and watch that?'

'It was only supposed to be…' He shook his head, not knowing where to go from here. 'How did you get here?' he tried instead.

'Never you mind,' she snapped. 'Sam said I was never to tell anyone. Such nice soldiers. They had me here before breakfast.'

He might have known. Ruby had her own means of getting where she wanted, when she wanted. And he wasn't off the hook yet.

'I would have come before,' she said, darkly

glowering. 'But I was babysitting Pierce's children. There I was, stuck with four kiddies, when I opened this week's *Woman's Journal*—it has the best macramé patterns—and there you were! And there was Rose, bending over a whole litter of piglets, and I knew the moment I saw her that this wasn't a paper contract. Then I had to wait for Pierce to get home and for Sam to organise transport before I could come. And I missed it.'

She fixed him with a look that said, 'stay right here; I'll deal with you later'. And she turned to Rose.

But Rose was facing her own demons. Julianna.

It *was* Julianna, but she was barely recognisable.

This wasn't the elegant young woman Nick had met the first night they'd been in the country. Julianna was dressed in quality trousers and blouse, as she had been that night, but that was as far as the elegance went. A savage bruise marred her left eye. Something had hit her hard. Her hair, twisted into an elegant chignon the last time Nick had seen her, was now a riot of unmanaged curls. Her face was blotched from weeping, and rivulets of mascara had edged down her cheeks. She looked much older than Rose, he thought. Drawn. Haggard.

'Rose, I never meant…' she was saying, while Rose kept staring at her like she was seeing a ghost.

'Never meant what?' she whispered.

'Last night. I swear, I didn't know. I thought…'

'What are you talking about?' Rose asked, and Julianna choked on a sob, reached for her sister's hands, but then seemed to think better of it. She retreated, backing against the table, holding to the table edge for support.

'I thought Jacques had given up,' she whispered. 'He said we'd go to Paris—he said we'd skimmed all we needed and the panel was never going to come down on our side. Rose, I married Jacques when I was seventeen. I know that's no excuse, and I could have left him, but I kept hoping things would be better. I thought I loved him. I never—'

'You wanted to rule,' Rose said bluntly, and Julianna blenched even further.

'From the time I was little our father told me it was my right. He said I was the one. He made it sound so wonderful, and I always felt the chosen one. But of course there was always Keifer and Konrad, and ruling seemed impossible. Only now it turns out Jacques knew Konrad would die young. Because—'

She faltered, then took a deep breath and continued, forcing every word out as if she could scarcely bear it. 'I swear I didn't know, but maybe our father knew. I think now that's why Jacques married me.'

'Oh, Jules.'

'What did your father know?' Erhard asked, but she shook her head. Whatever had to be said must be said in her own time.

'I knew by the time Konrad died that Jacques didn't love me,' she said, and she tilted her chin in a gesture that mirrored Rose's. 'I've been so miserable, I just stopped…seeing. When Erhard came to see me after Konrad was killed, I told him that Jacques could do what he wanted with the country. I didn't care.'

They were all focused on her now. Ruby had turned from Nick and was looking at Julianna with a look Nick recognised. Ruby had raised seven foster-sons. When a new boy had arrived at her home, this was the look she'd used.

Here was a chick that needed a mother hen, her look said. But Julianna was in her late twenties.

'You sound like you have that depression thing,' Ruby said sympathetically. 'I had it after my husband died. It was like I was in a fog, and the fog was too thick to push through.'

'I did,' Julianna said, choking on a sob. 'I do. Last week, after that awful time with the crowd, we went to Paris. But then yesterday Jacques said we had to come back. He said we weren't coming to the wedding, but we had to be near.'

'Why?' Erhard asked, and she put her hands to her face again as if she couldn't bear to go on.

'He didn't tell me,' she whispered. 'He's stopped telling me anything. I think he's even stopped thinking I can hear. It's my stupid fault. It's just been easier to agree, to do what he says, to be left alone.'

'Only last night…' Erhard prodded.

'He was excited,' Julianna whispered. 'We were staying in one of the palace hunting-lodges, which was weird, all on its own. But I wasn't thinking. Or maybe I *was* thinking—of you, Rose, and your wedding, and how you were my sister and you were being married and I wasn't there.'

'You weren't either?' Ruby said, and sniffed her disgust. 'I might have known.'

'I went to bed,' Julianna said, too miserable to be deflected. 'But I heard him downstairs, pacing, pacing. And then I started thinking. The fog lifted a little. I heard him on the phone saying we were only twenty miles away and we could be at the palace in an hour. And of course there'd be suspicions, but the money transfer was impossible to trace and there was no proof. And hadn't he succeeded with Konrad? A car crash with a drunk driver, he said, and he sounded really pleased with himself. No proof at all. And then Erhard…'

She looked wildly at Erhard, as if she couldn't believe he could be here. 'He said to whoever it was, "But you should have done better with Fritz.

The old man turned up today. You were meant to hit him so hard he'd never stick his nose into what's not his business again." He had you bashed. He…'

'He didn't,' Erhard said gently, reluctantly. 'His thugs came to my home two weeks ago. My wife's poodle raised the alarm. They killed our Chloe, but Hilda and I managed to escape.' He closed his eyes, remembering the terror, but then he looked directly at Rose and then at Nick.

'I'm sorry,' he said. 'I should have told you. I thought with all the publicity he'd never try to hurt you two. I so wanted this wedding to go ahead. I took Hilda out of the country because she was terrified. I reassured her. But I didn't think he'd try…I misjudged.'

'We all misjudged,' Julianna whispered. 'I never thought he would, but he did. Jacques did. "We'll get away with them both," he told the guy on the end of the phone. I knew what he was saying. He'd killed Konrad and he was going to kill Rose and Nick.'

There was an appalled silence. Julianna was staring blindly at Rose. 'You're my sister, Rose,' she whispered. 'I can't get away from that. When I thought of what he was planning…'

She swallowed, fighting for the energy to go on. 'Finally I went downstairs and asked him,' she managed. 'Even then I couldn't believe he'd go that far. But he just looked at me as if I was stupid, as if I was nothing. And then he hit me.'

'Oh, my dear,' Ruby whispered.

'He pulled me back up to the bedroom and locked me in,' Julianna said dully. 'He ripped out my phone extension. He said I was in it up to my neck, and if I said a word I'd go down first. And I couldn't get out. I tried and I yelled, but he laughed and told me to take a tranquillizer. Take five, he yelled. And then the phone rang down-stairs. I heard Jacques say one word: "Well?" That's all. Then silence.'

She swallowed, and Nick could see the horrors of the night were still with her. 'I was sick,' she whispered. 'I thought it was over.' She took a jagged breath and looked at Rose as if she still couldn't believe her sister could still be alive. 'Then the front door slammed and I heard his car. The lodge-keeper came by this morning and let me out, but Jacques was gone. I rang here and they said you were safe, but I had to see. The lodge-keeper brought me here.' She shook her head as if trying to shake away a nightmare. 'Rose, I swear I didn't know what he intended. I'd never…I'd never…'

'I know you wouldn't,' Rose said softly. Ruby moved aside—as Ruby would; the woman had the most finely tuned intuition Nick had ever known—and Rose took Julianna's hands.

'Even last night, when Nick said it had to be Jacques, I still knew it couldn't be you,' Rose said softly. 'You're my sister.'

'Oh God,' Julianna said, and she pulled back and put her face in her hands. 'What must you all think of me? I don't want this. I hate it. I want to be out. I want to be ordinary. I want to go somewhere, breed horses, take in washing, anything but this. I don't want to be royal.'

'Taking in washing's a bit extreme,' Rose said, and Julianna choked on something between laughter and a sob.

'I don't care. But how can I do anything? Jacques will never let me.'

'No one owns you,' Rose said. 'I'm just figuring that out. You need to do what you need to do. As for the royal bit—can't you resign?'

'You can't just resign.'

'Edward did,' Rose said. 'Back in England. With Mrs Simpson. Isn't that right? He was supposed to be king, but he signed something that said he was giving up his rights to the throne. Erhard, can't Julianna resign?'

'I don't know.' The old man looked grey. He groped blindly for a chair, and Nick pulled one forward for him.

There was too much emotion here, Nick thought. If he wasn't careful Erhard would collapse. He strode out through the conservatory doors to the sitting room beyond. There were decanters on the sideboard. He poured a generous brandy for the old man and carried it back.

Erhard hardly registered when he placed it in his fingers. 'I should have warned you of the dangers,' he whispered. 'I wanted this wedding to go ahead so much.'

'Drink a little,' Nick urged. 'And don't look like you've just confessed murder. We have our assassin from last night under lock and key, and everything else palls into insignificance.' He shook his head. 'And you've lost your dog. I suspect Rose will say there's nothing so dreadful.'

Erhard looked up at him, and Nick smiled. He put a hand on the old man's shoulder and squeezed.

'We're here now. We're alive. We'll find Jacques.'

'And you'll tell me the truth,' Ruby said. Nick's foster mother had been quiet for a whole five minutes now—almost a course record—but it seemed she'd been talking aside to Rose urgently. 'Rose tells me this wedding *is* a fraud. A marriage of convenience.'

'Rose?' he said helplessly, and Rose shrugged and tried to smile.

'Why not be honest? It is a fraud.'

'But…'

'That's what you called it this morning,' she said.

He had. But last night… Over and over the image played in his head. Rose standing in her bare feet and chemise, aiming her gun with her eyes filled with terror.

Rose against the world. Rose with bumblebees. Rose in his arms.

But Rose was moving on. 'If Julianna is resigning, then I could too,' she said, attempting to sound brisk and businesslike. 'I've just thought—if neither Julianna or I will take the crown, then Nick is Crown Prince. Which makes sense. My father wasn't really royal, and you want it, don't you, Nick?'

Did he want it? Suddenly they were all looking at him, and the question hung.

Of course he did. This had started as something that seemed exciting, almost as a Boy's Own adventure. But somewhere in there…

'My mother was a princess here,' he said slowly. 'She was so homesick. She'd want me to take it on..'

'There you go, then,' Rose said. 'You can do it.'

'But together,' Ruby said urgently, sensing trouble. 'Because you're married.'

'No.' Nick took a deep breath. 'Maybe it's time for Rose not to be married.'

Ruby sighed. She put her hands on her hips and surveyed him with care.

'Right,' she said at last. 'You know, I'm getting

really muddled here. Didn't you just get married yesterday?'

'Yes, but Rose didn't want to get married,' he explained. 'She did it out of obligation. Rose has had too many obligations for too long. Like Julianna, she needs to be free. If Julianna's prepared to renounce her succession too, then it leaves Rose free to do what she likes. We can have the marriage annulled and she can renounce her succession too, if she wishes.'

'I have a feeling the people in this country are going to get very confused,' Ruby said darkly. 'If I'm anything to go by, they'll be very confused indeed.'

'Maybe they'll kick Nick out,' Rose said. The group seemed to be reviving now. Just a little. Rose's words contained just a trace of her old perkiness.

He loved that about her. He loved her to distraction. How could he let her go?

He could let her go, because he loved her.

'You know, they might,' Julianna said, breaking back into the conversation. She was suddenly tremulously hopeful. She'd faced the nightmare and come out the other side. 'The riot when we put you under house-arrest was frightening. I've never seen anything like it. Until then I hadn't realised… Maybe I still don't realise what power the throne has.'

'I can't see Nick taking on the throne alone,' Erhard said.

Ruby had been concentrating really, really hard. She still looked confused, but she wasn't prepared to be relegated to the role of mere onlooker yet.

'Nick will do whatever needs doing,' she declared. 'He's a very responsible boy.'

'Yeah?' That was Rose. She'd been hugging Julianna, but her attention was caught by that. Her eyes flew to Nick's. 'Responsible—is he just? Well, well. I'd never have thought it.'

And suddenly she smiled, then gave him a measured look which was suddenly all about who'd remembered the condom last night. It was like the sun had come out. After all this emotion, after all this fear, she was suddenly teasing him.

He'd never realised he could blush.

'Why don't you want the throne?' Julianna asked Rose.

'I suspect no one's asked Rose what she's wanted for a very long time,' Ruby said, putting her oar in again. 'Did you know her mother- and father-in-law were trying to make her have babies with her dead husband's sperm?'

No one knew what to say to that. Especially Nick. He stared at Ruby. Then he stared at Rose. Appalled. 'Is this true?'

Rose nodded, her eyes suspiciously bright. 'Yes, but how Ruby found out…'

'I found out exactly the same way as Monsieur Fritz found out about Nick,' Ruby said with asperity. 'My friend Eloise at my macramé club told me she'd been talking to someone who was asking about you, Nick. So I did the same. I have a friend who lives in your district in Yorkshire, Rose, and I got an in-depth report of what you've been going through. You've been bullied into taking over your poor husband's life, and now you've been bullied into taking over this one. Enough.'

'I chose.' Rose ventured.

'The worst of two alternatives,' Nick said slowly, watching her. And suddenly things were clear. Or as clear as they could be in the circumstances. She should never have been asked to do this, he thought. In all of this, that she'd been asked to take on more responsibility…

'Why did you ask Rose?' he said to Erhard, and there was something in his voice that made them all turn to him. 'Rose's father thought Rose wasn't royal. You've inferred Julianna wasn't Eric's legitimate child either. You've said the DNA thing isn't an issue, but maybe it could be. You didn't go down that path. Why not? Shouldn't I have been the one to take responsibility?'

'But I didn't know you,' Erhard said bluntly.

'You didn't know Rose.'

'I did.' Erhard was still clutching his brandy

glass as if he needed it, but a little colour had crept back. 'Rose was here until she was fifteen. She was always the reliable one. Her mother was ill. Her father was a drunk. The old Prince was failing. She took everything on her shoulders, worrying about everything. When I enquired about her, it seemed she'd kept right on doing that in Yorkshire. She was responsible, and that was what I wanted.'

'You wanted Rose to keep on taking the burden.'

'I didn't think.'

'No,' Nick said gently. 'We couldn't expect you to be thinking of Rose's welfare. You were frightened for your country and you wanted what was best. Rose is the best. We all know that. But it's time someone looked out for her interests. That time is now, and that someone is me.'

Rose was looking confused. He reached out and tugged her against him, feeling almost compelled to hold her close. But he wouldn't hold her. He mustn't.

He loved her too much.

'So here's the plan,' he said softly, feeling Rose mould to his body, loving the feel of her, but knowing he had to offer her freedom. 'Julianna, you abdicate. We'll do our best to find Jacques and put him in jail, but maybe for the time being you could go home with Ruby.'

He smiled at Ruby. 'I know. You're annoyed with

me, but I'm asking for your help, and when have you ever refused it? Ruby lives in Dolphin Bay, which is the best place in the world to recuperate. Maybe, Erhard, you could go too. You're looking ill. There are two wonderful doctors at Dolphin Bay.' He grinned. 'And there are all sorts of weird and wonderful dogs. If you take your wife, I'll guarantee you come home with a new puppy.'

'And Rose?' Ruby asked, sounding wary. Not hostile to his plan, though, just thoughtful.

'I think Rose should go too,' he said.

'I'm not going anywhere,' Rose said, stiffening.

'You must.'

'Oh, sure. And leave you here to get yourself killed?'

'Well, that won't happen,' Ruby said, still sounding thoughtful. 'I've organised that.'

'You have?' Nick blinked.

'You're not the only one who can organise,' Ruby retorted. 'This is a mess. People going round at midnight shooting other people...I brought my boys up to be responsible citizens, which is why they're all flying in tonight.'

'All?'

'Pierce will be a bit longer because he's coming from Australia,' she said. 'Sam couldn't go back to fetch him. But when I got here this morning and found out about the shooting I said enough, I need all my boys. So they'll be here. Sam's taking security over right now—Monsieur Fritz has set it up for him, and Sam swears we'll have this Jacques person locked up by lunchtime. Blake's got the legal mind. Darcy can sort out the army. Between them they'll have this place sorted, and then it'll be time for Rose to decide whether she wants to come back again.'

'I don't…' Rose tried, but Nick smiled and shook his head.

'You're trying to argue with Ruby?'

'I'm not leaving you,' she said.

'You don't need to worry,' Ruby said. 'I realise Nick is a very good-looking boy, and he has a very nice smile, but he's got to give you time to think. Don't worry about him being lonely—his brothers will be here.'

'But I can't afford—'

'You can afford,' Nick said, feeling gutted, but knowing he had to let her go. 'I've looked into the royal exchequer this week. For all the poverty in the country, the royal fortune is practically obscene. I want to plough some of that into capital works to get the economy going, but there's more than enough to let you and Julianna spend the rest of your lives in comfort. You can take that trip around Australia you wanted to do. You can do anything you want. You have no responsibilities, Rose. Not one.'

There was a moment's stunned pause.

'So I'm free,' Rose said. 'When I said I could resign…' She swallowed. 'I didn't think. And I couldn't take Hoppy—or not straight away.'

'Who's Hoppy?' Ruby asked, and Rose motioned to the little dog who'd been standing in the background looking innocuous. As well he might. He'd come via the kitchens where he'd been given a rather large ham-bone leftover from the festivities of the day before. He was paying attention to the goings on—but only just.

'There's quarantine regulations in Australia,' Rose said. 'I can't leave my dog. So…' She took a deep breath. 'I do have a responsibility.'

'Nick will look after your dog,' Ruby said.

'Nick's not very responsible,' Rose retorted.

'You should know,' Nick said, and smiled. 'You're my wife.'

'You said it was a sham marriage,' Ruby said sharply, looking from one to the other.

'That was Nick,' Rose said.

'Do you want it to be?' Nick asked. 'Sham, that is?'

'I haven't learned to swim yet,' she said, and she was smiling tremulously, as if she was about to take a very large step and wasn't quite sure if it was in the right direction.

'So it's not sham?' Ruby said.

'Ask Nick what I have on my knickers,' Rose whispered.

'Bumblebees,' Nick said promptly.

'And my wedding knickers?'

'Butterflies.'

'There you go, then,' Rose said. 'How sham is that?'

There was a loaded silence. No one said a word.

'You know,' Ruby said finally, looking vaguely into middle distance, yet not looking at anyone at all. 'I could really use a brandy. It was very inconsiderate of Nick to bring one for Erhard and not for me. I'm a frail old lady and I need my sustenance. Julianna. Erhard. If you were to take an arm each, I might just be able to stagger feebly forth and find my own brandy.'

'You're sure they're safe to leave alone?' Erhard asked, but he was smiling.

'They're talking bumblebees and butterflies,' Ruby said. 'Unless you're interested in botany, I have a feeling this conversation is going to get really, really boring.'

CHAPTER ELEVEN

THEY were left alone. Apart from Hoppy, who'd gone back to bone munching.

Nick was aware that it behoved him to tread warily. *Very* warily. There was so much at stake.

He had to forget the bumblebees and start from scratch, he decided. Repeat the conversation they'd just had, and hope he got the same outcome.

Had he got an outcome? He found his heart was having trouble beating. Maybe because he was having trouble breathing. So much depended on these next few minutes.

'That was frivolous,' he said, and she nodded.

'Yes.'

'So we need to be businesslike.'

'Yes.'

'I'm not sure where to start,' he said, which seemed a good sort of start. It was the best he could do under the circumstances.

'Start by telling me that you still want this job,'

Rose said, being brisk. Trying not to smile. 'And tell me why.'

He hesitated. 'Rose, I didn't think this through,' he admitted. 'Yes, it appealed, that I could do a bit of good. And it seemed an amazing offer—to be Prince Consort—to spend a few weeks here and get off scot-free.'

'But…'

'There's the "but",' he said. 'It had to happen and it has. I can't walk away now. I'm in too deep. The kid who rescued Hoppy is depending on us—on me—as are his parents, and his aunts and uncles, and his whole extended family. The country's a mess and it can be put to rights. I want that job, Rose, and I intend to take it.'

'So I really can walk away?' she said, wondering.

'It's up to you. I told you. There's more than enough money in the royal coffers to provide well for you and for Julianna. There's no need to be a princess to have a life of ease. You deserve the choice.' He smiled. 'Julianna won't have to take in that washing after all.'

'I don't want a life of ease,' she said.

'You wanted to travel around Australia. You told me that. I figure this gives you the freedom to do it. I'll be Prince Regent. When you've done with your travelling, maybe you can come back, decide whether or not to take on the throne, and I can leave or stay, whatever you wish.'

'But that puts your life in limbo.'

'No,' he said forcibly. 'I want this job, Rose. There's so much I can do. There are so many plans to make—so much to do to get the economy turned round. It's the most exciting job I've ever taken on—it's an honour to be asked to take it.'

'But…' she said.

'But?'

'I wouldn't mind helping.'

'You can at the end of the year. Or you can now. You can take over in your own right.'

'I'm not a legitimate princess.'

'You're the acknowledged daughter of a prince. You're my wife. You're legitimate in every sense of the word.'

'It was a fake marriage.'

'We signed all the documents,' he said. 'It felt real to me.' He smiled. 'And you've personally introduced your botany collection to the world. There'll not be one person in this castle who'll believe our marriage is sham now.'

'But you don't want me to stay…with *you*.' It was a soft whisper, but behind it… Was he imagining it, or had there been a tiny thread of hope?

'You want to be free,' Nick said, trying not to let his heart leap. She couldn't want him. He had to be imagining it. Theirs was a marriage of convenience.

But, damn it, he wasn't going to let her go without giving it a shot.

'Though I wouldn't mind,' he said softly. 'If you wanted to stay. I mean, freedom means freedom of choice, so there is that option.'

'Freedom does mean choice,' she whispered back. 'So if I chose, say, not to travel round Australia but instead maybe to travel, say, round the perimeter of this castle...With my dog and my companion.'

'What sort of companion?'

'Ooh. Maybe a husband?'

The world stilled. The world held its breath.

'What about that for an idea?' she said cautiously. 'In theory, are there things about it that might appeal to you?'

'There might be,' he said, just as cautiously.

'Like, um, what?'

'Sharing a tent is always fun,' he said.

The smile was returning to her eyes. It was the smile he'd fallen for.

He smiled back, and for Rose it was the same. Nick's was the smile that had lifted her from the bleakness of her past and propelled her into the future.

'There's probably room in the grounds of the royal castle for a small tent,' she told him. 'But we'd have to get your brother's security forces to leave us be. Floodlights in the wee small hours sweeping our tent might not be as romantic as I'd like.'

'You'd like it to be romantic?'

'Wouldn't you?'

His smile died. The look he gave her was searching. He wasn't touching her. Why not? She wanted so badly to be touched.

She couldn't reach out to him. She wouldn't. A girl had some pride.

'Rose, your freedom.'

'What about your freedom?' she asked. 'You never wanted to be married.'

'I never wanted to be married to anyone at all until I met you. Now I never want to be married to anyone *but* you. But I won't hold you, Rose.'

'I want to be held.'

'You've never been free.'

'Freedom's got some downsides. It needs some inclusions.'

'Like what?'

'You.'

There it was. Out in front, for both of them to see.

And his smile didn't fade one bit. It changed, deepened, broadened, and the smile in his eyes was a caress all by itself.

'I love you, Rose,' he said simply, and her heart did that stupid stopping thing all over again. He'd said it. She looked deep into his eyes and saw immutable truth: love and wonder and need. But also a trace of bleakness—even fear—as though even now he felt like he was exposing himself. A child who'd been brought up in foster homes. Who'd struggled to be independent. Who'd struggled not to need, and who'd come to the same sweet conclusion that she had.

That need wasn't such a bad thing. In fact, need could be the most glorious thing in the world.

'How can you love me?' she managed, and he smiled.

'In a million ways. Far too many to count. But Rose, your freedom…'

'I am free,' she told him. 'I'm free to go wherever I want in the world. I'm free to leave the shadows of Max behind, and move forward without guilt or regret. You've given me that. I'm not sure how, and I'm not sure why, but you have. I'm free to be my own woman and I'm free to love. And I do love, Nick. I choose to love you.'

'You do?'

'Yes.'

Still he didn't move. It was like he couldn't believe what he was hearing.

'We'll have to live here.'

'Oh, no. A castle. In the most beautiful country in the world.' She smiled up at him, feeling dizzy with happiness. 'I'll try to bear it.'

'We'll be in the public eye. It's a goldfish bowl, royalty.'

'It might be fun,' she said, with a certainty that was becoming stronger by the minute. 'I felt claustrophobic here as a kid, but I'd have a lot more freedom now. Us in our tent on the front lawn…I expect we'd shock the socks off the tabloid press at least once a week.'

'I'll never ask you to have babies.'

She stilled. There was so much between them. Why was he not holding her?

'You won't?' she whispered.

'Rose, to be asked to bear Max's baby…'

'It was different,' she said, thinking it through, trying to figure things out for herself. 'It was just… It just felt wrong. You know, Max had that sperm frozen when he was seventeen years old. He never discussed it with me. It was like a bolt from the blue. If I'd had a baby, it would have been like bearing a child that belonged to Max's past. And any baby I have I want to belong to the future. So if you and I wanted a baby…'

'I never thought I would,' he said softly, wondrously. 'I never imagined I could possibly want to bring a child into the world. But you know, with you… If we had a castle…'

'And Ruby as a grandma. She'd make a great grandma.'

'She will.' His smile was back now, with vengeance. 'And maybe we could even include Gladys and Bob. Just a little bit.'

'You'd do that?'

'I'll talk to them,' he said. 'If you want. They've been part of your life for so long that it might hurt if they don't give us their blessing.' He frowned. 'Maybe some of that independence money you've just knocked back could set up a fund for a veterinarian practice in the town—in Max's name.'

'Oh, Nick,' she said, awed.

'I know,' he said softly, and grinned. 'I'm wonderful.'

'And handsome and kind and clever.'

'And *humble*,' he said. 'Don't forget humble.'

'I'll give you humble,' she said and glowered, and her glower was so delicious that he chuckled.

'Rose?'

'Yes?'

'Most of all I want you,' he said.

'Nick?'

'Yes?'

'If you don't kiss me right this minute I might do something I might regret.'

'What might that be?'

'I might have to kiss you first,' she said, and it was a near thing. A very near thing. Who kissed who?

Rose didn't know. She didn't care. She fell into Nick's arms, and he kissed her until her toes curled.

While at the glass doors of the conservatory three people stood and watched this second wedding-ceremony. The joining of this man to this woman to become man and wife.

'I did get to see it after all,' Ruby said, and smiled and smiled.

'And there's the coronation to come,' Erhard said, deeply satisfied.

'And maybe…' Julianna smiled through the glass at her sister, and then turned to usher the two oldies away. After all, what was a sister for but to protect her sibling?

'Maybe there'll be the odd christening to come too,' she said softly. 'I think the succession to the throne of Alp de Montez is assured. And I think we can safely leave them to it.'

Celebrate 100 years of pure reading pleasure with Mills & Boon®

To mark our centenary, each month we're
publishing a special 100th Birthday Edition.
These celebratory editions are packed with extra
features and include a FREE bonus story.

Now that's worth celebrating!

4th January 2008

The Vanishing Viscountess by Diane Gaston
With FREE story The Mysterious Miss M
*This award-winning tale of the Regency Underworld
launched Diane Gaston's writing career.*

1st February 2008

Cattle Rancher, Secret Son by Margaret Way
With FREE story His Heiress Wife
Margaret Way excels at rugged Outback heroes…

15th February 2008

Raintree: Inferno by Linda Howard
With FREE story Loving Evangeline
*A double dose of Linda Howard's heady mix of
passion and adventure.*

Don't miss out! From February you'll have the
chance to enter our fabulous monthly prize draw.
See special 100th Birthday Editions for details.

www.millsandboon.co.uk

0108/CENTENARY_2-IN-1

FREE!

4 Books
and a surprise gift!

We would like to take this opportunity to thank you for reading this Mills & Boon® book by offering you the chance to take FOUR more specially selected titles from the Romance series absolutely FREE! We're also making this offer to introduce you to the benefits of the Mills & Boon® Reader Service™—

- ★ FREE home delivery
- ★ FREE gifts and competitions
- ★ FREE monthly Newsletter
- ★ Exclusive Reader Service offers
- ★ Books available before they're in the shops

Accepting these FREE books and gift places you under no obligation to buy, you may cancel at any time, even after receiving your free shipment. Simply complete your details below and return the entire page to the address below. You don't even need a stamp!

YES! Please send me 4 free Romance books and a surprise gift. I understand that unless you hear from me, I will receive 6 superb new titles every month for just £2.99 each, postage and packing free. I am under no obligation to purchase any books and may cancel my subscription at any time. The free books and gift will be mine to keep in any case.

N8ZEF

Ms/Mrs/Miss/Mr .... Initials ....
                                                        BLOCK CAPITALS PLEASE
Surname ....
Address ....

....

.... Postcode ....

Send this whole page to:
UK: FREEPOST CN81, Croydon, CR9 3WZ